LAST KNOWN PSITION

LAST KNOWN

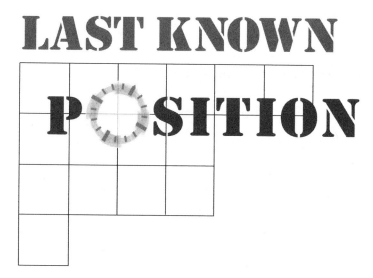

POSITION

BY JAMES MATHEWS

2008 WINNER, KATHERINE ANNE PORTER PRIZE IN SHORT FICTION

University of North Texas Press
Denton, Texas

©2008 James Mathews

10 9 8 7 6 5 4 3 2 1

Permissions:
University of North Texas Press
P.O. Box 311336
Denton, TX 76203-1336

∞The paper used in this book meets the minimum requirements of the American National Standard for Permanence of Paper for Printed Library Materials, z39.48.1984. Binding materials have been chosen for durability.

Library of Congress Cataloging-in-Publication Data

Mathews, James, 1965–
  Last known position / by James Mathews.
    p. cm.
  "2008 Winner, Katherine Anne Porter Prize in Short Fiction."
  ISBN 978-1-57441-252-9 (pbk. : alk. paper)
  I. Title.
  PS3613.A8433L37 2008
  813'.6—dc22
                    2008028290

Last Known Position is Number 7 in the Katherine Anne Porter Prize in Short Fiction Series

Text design by Carol Sawyer/Rose Design

For Diana

CONTENTS

ACKNOWLEDGMENTS

I have had the privilege of sharing many of the following stories with friends who also happen to be gifted writers. Among them are Jack McEnany, Delores Martín, James Beane, Carmelinda Blagg, Dana Cann, Catherine Bell, Madelyn Rosenberg, and Kathleen Wheaton. Where the stories are successful can usually be traced to a kind, but firm elbow-shot to the ribs from one or most of these writers.

When and where the stories touch on military issues— in particular "Seven Rifles at Dawn"—a shout-out goes to my brothers in the 113th Wing, DC Air National Guard. Serving with you guys has been an honor and pleasure and if we're ever called up again, you know I've got your six. IYAAYAS!

"Grenade" was first published in *Beacon Street Review* (now *Redivider*).

"Roar" was first published in *The Northwest Review* and was noted as a "Distinguished Mystery Story" in the *2004 Best American Mystery Stories*.

"The Fifth Week" was first published in *The Wisconsin Review*.

"Last Known Position: 2,000 Feet Above the World and Descending" was first published in *The Heartland Review.*

"Strong Arm" was first published in *The Roanoke Review.*

"Seven Rifles at Dawn" was first published in the *Timber Creek Review.*

"Man Swallows Goldfish While Sleepwalking, Chokes to Death" was first published in *The Madison Review.*

"Cannibals in the Basement" was first published in *The Greensboro Review.*

"Our Deepest Sympathies" was first published in *Wilmington Blues.*

GRENADE

Trace Mullins stole an M67 fragmentation grenade from his father—the post weapons range instructor who, according to Trace, had "a whole closet full of stuff"—and we all spent one Saturday afternoon in the dugouts behind the Officer's Club pool deciding what we were going to blow up. It was the beginning of our last summer vacation on Ft. Bliss, deep in the heart of Texas. Well, maybe not the heart. More like the intestinal tract. The four of us—Trace, Danny Ticker, Marvin Woods, and myself—were still a month away from enlisting in the Army, each one as invulnerable and bored as every other recent high school graduate on the planet. But even though we'd done everything there was to do (in our minds), we still couldn't shake the feeling that we'd be spending the rest of our lives patting at our pockets, as if for a lost key, unable to pinpoint that one vital reward we missed out on. Such misconceptions have watered the weeds of not a few epic disasters.

"Symbolism is important here," Trace said. He was picking at the steel loop that dangled from the cotter pin of the grenade. "This baby has to speak. I don't want to just blow up a trashcan."

He passed the grenade to Danny who cupped it with both hands, as if receiving a communion wafer. "Wow," Danny said, his voice catching. "It's light."

"Until you pull the pin," Trace said. "Then you're holding a shot put." He leaned back and stared out at the softball diamond, muddied from a recent rainstorm. "That's what my old man says anyway." His eyes were dark gray, like gunpowder, dashed with just enough wisdom to be threatening. A weary fly made the mistake of lazing across his line of sight and he snatched it out of the air with the reflexes of a coiled snake. When he opened his hand, the dead insect floated to the ground like a piece of balled-up black thread.

On the dugout bench beside him, Marvin unfurled a plastic baggie of purple-haired sensimilla he had scored from a GI over in the enlisted barracks. "We should toss it into the O Club lounge," he offered, "when all the butter bars come charging in for their evening coma."

Trace glanced over at me and said, "That would be mercy killing. They don't deserve mercy."

"Isn't it supposed to be shaped like a pineapple?" Danny said. His eyes looked wet and swollen with awe. He was the youngest among us, as thin as a refugee, with a clean, pert voice that puberty forgot. He was also the most intelligent, which meant, logically, that he was most likely to come to great harm. His father was a helicopter pilot who had a reputation for beating up the family, especially Danny's mother, a South Korean national who spoke little to no English. We used to joke that the only clear phrase she knew was "Operator, get me MPs!"

"You're talking World War II," Trace told him wisely. "These babies are much, much meaner. Bigger blast radius. Higher kill rate."

"Won't your old man miss it?" I asked him.

Trace shook his head. "Plenty more where this came from, Cadet, don't you worry."

"I wasn't."

He went on to explain that he didn't mean to imply his theft was without risk. His father would be out for blood if he found out, but the only way he'd find out was if somebody told. If that happened, Trace assured us, that somebody would be getting pay-back. That somebody would get a grenade for Christmas. Or a birthday. Whichever came first.

"I say we sabotage the Bradley parade next week," Marvin suggested. "We could roll it into the street when the Army band marches by." He giggled nervously, focusing what little concentration he could muster toward packing weed into a bong constructed out of a pickle jar. He always giggled, usually without provocation, with a looseness that I likened to a cheap doll after it had been shaken a few times. The dugout quickly grew hazy with smoke as the bong made its way among us.

"Or that horse," Trace said, his eyes softened with a slight buzz. "I'm so sick of hearing about that goddamn horse. Last night, I dreamt I was married to it."

We all nodded in stoned agreement. Every summer, the post commander organized a parade to show off the latest military hardware he was in charge of. This year, the bash was in honor of what would have been the one-hundredth birthday of General of the Army Omar Bradley. Bradley was, of course, dead, but a parade horse he once rode was being flown in from California. There were banners all over the base announcing the event.

"Wait a minute, hold it, no way," Danny blurted, wasting a mouthful of perfectly good pot smoke. He looked startled, a full minute or so behind in the discussion. He pushed the grenade back into Trace's hands. "I'm not going to be a part of anyone get-ting hurt. Forget it. You can just cut me right the hell out if that's your plan." He made it sound like a threat, although he must have known that it would never have occurred to us to feel threatened by him.

"Stop crying," Trace told him.

"I'm not crying. My dad's going to be in that parade."

"So's mine. Look hard and tell me if you see me crying." Trace turned to me. "So how about it, Cadet? How bad should we be?" He handed me the grenade as if this would clarify things, as if I could make no decision without first consulting, like a crystal ball, the explosive device.

I examined the grenade. A seamless olive drab orb save for the metal housing unit and safety lever, roughly the size of a tangerine, comfortable in my hand. Although lightweight, I could tell immediately what Trace had meant by shot put. The responsibility of taking hold of something that could turn us into hamburger in a burst of brutal light settled into the sinew and cartilage of my knuckles, pushing sweat into my hand like grease through a sieve.

Feeling Trace's eyes on me, I pursed my lips, turning the grenade over a couple times as though looking for imperfections. I didn't want him to see my unease, to get hold of it. Since the day we'd met two years before, I stood somewhat in awe of Trace, the intense and troublesome sergeant major's son, just the kind of friend my mother warned me about. He didn't return the sentiment though. He disliked me at first because my father was an officer. Worse, a *medical* officer. Because of this, he enjoyed baiting me to no end. He especially liked calling me "Cadet" despite the fact that I had sworn I would enlist. Over time, neither of us demanded too much of the other. Our relationship was somehow simplified by the fact that we were destined to come to blows.

I looked up and found the three of them staring at me, waiting for my answer, the final vote in our grimly hatched scheme. Finally, for lack of anything resembling a courageous thought, I said to them: "Let's kill something."

Trace laughed greedily through a veil of smoke, pleased with my answer. "Or someone," he said. He plucked the grenade from my hand, then offered up a gamy, fluoridated smile for Danny to show that he was kidding—sort of.

It was the last time I ever saw him smile.

With the grenade nested safely in a camouflaged TDY pack slung over his shoulder, Trace led us down Sheridan Road, single file, in step and silent, like soldiers on patrol. Off our left shoulders, the desert sun kissed the spine of the Franklin Mountains, stretching our shadows to obscene twelve-foot lengths. There wasn't a cloud to be seen above, which was hard to believe since only hours before, a storm had dumped probably half the annual rainfall in about fifteen minutes.

As we shuffled ever forward, past the movie theater and Four Seasons, I couldn't help but notice the stark decline in housing quality. The officer's quarters, where I lived, slowly gave way to post enlisted. These houses were decidedly smaller, red-bricked and screenless, with none of the clipped, pampered hedges found on my part of the base. My mother called this area "the projects," something I never repeated to my three friends although I'd heard them say it once or twice.

Just before the dreary duplexes yielded to the parade fields on the north end of base, Trace held up his hand and we stopped with staggered imprecision. He tiptoed a few feet, then squatted beside a swath of sagebrush that framed one of the grassless backyards, reached in and retrieved a medium-sized yellow cat. He stood up, cradling the complacent animal against his chest, all the while whispering into its ear, "Who's dat? Who's dat whittle kitty?"

"Look-ee there, Danny," Marvin said, feigning awe. "I thought your mama-san fricasseed up all the cats on this street."

Danny ignored the gibe. "That's Pontoon. He belongs to my next door—"

"Nobody asked you who he belongs to, soldier," Trace snapped. He flashed us all a feral look that demanded obedience, or at least ignorance, then headed off toward the parade field, scratching the cat's head to calm it.

Marvin offered a subdued giggle and gave Danny a playful prod as we fell back into line. "Yeah, nobody asked you, soldier boy."

The parade field was deserted, but showed signs of looming activity, including a red, white and blue cloth banner draped along the front of the grandstand. Beneath the podium was a giant circus poster with the caption, *Ft. Bliss Welcomes "Reveille," General Omar Bradley's Favorite Parade Horse!*

Marvin giggled and delivered his best Gomer Pyle, "Gaaawwlee, did you guys know that General Bradley's favorite parade horse is gonna be in the parade? Didya know? Huh, didya?"

"He does tricks," Danny said.

"Now what I can't figure out," Marvin went on, reverting to his own voice which, come to think of it, didn't sound that much different from Gomer Pyle, "is how they got the old coot up in the saddle? I mean a horse only lives for so long and Bradley kicked the bucket, what, ten years ago? How could it be his favorite if he never rode it?"

"My dad met him once," I said.

"Who? Reveille?"

"Bradley, dip shit. It was right before he died. In Ft. Dix. My dad said the brass just couldn't get enough of the old guy." As we moved away from the parade field toward Pershing Drive, I related the story as my father had told it. Of how he and some fifty junior officers had been forced to study rules and regulations of formal military mess dining. Stuff like which spoon to use, when to use it, and what to use it on. After getting decked up in resplendent mess dress uniforms, complete with polished shoulder boards, the men took their seats around long white tables held down by a ton of silver. Called to attention, it was more shock than anything when the ancient, disease-riddled Bradley—Five-Star Omar, the Master of the Normandy Breakout, the GI's General—was wheel-chaired into the room by a pair of morose light colonels. Heavily sedated, my father had said. Stone cold stoned. The old guy wouldn't have known where he was if he knew where he was. Awe and anticipation gave way to repressed disgust as the aides began to feed the old man, spooning pea soup into his barely receptive mouth, dabbing at the run-off slithering down his bony chin.

I was about to relate what I had considered the best part of the story. How my father had written a letter of protest to the base commander, asking for the charades to discontinue. He'd even managed to convince several of his friends to co-sign the letter which, as one would expect from a well-oiled, spit-shined military unit, yielded nothing.

But Trace cut me off. "And to think," he said, over his shoulder, "we'll be missing all that by enlisting."

"Me, I can't wait 'til I'm that age," Marvin said. "Drooling and wetting myself. All them pretty nurses cleaning up after me."

"You're a sick pup," I told him, and he giggled appreciatively.

"Fifteen years," Danny piped in from the rear.

"What's that, shitbird?" Marvin said.

"The lifespan of a horse."

"Hey, do us a favor and keep up with the damn conversation."

"You wanted to know."

"Ten minutes ago I wanted to know. Is your brain that fried, man? Or is it because you're half commie?"

"My mom's *South* Korean, you fucker!" Danny shouted.

"Same island though, right?"

"It's a peninsula!"

"Quiet in the ranks," Trace sneered back at us, his fingers scratching the underside of the cat's chin. "You're scaring the prisoner."

We chuckled at him, the hesitant kind of chuckle one hears in anticipation of a punchline. Trace just kept on marching. We just kept on following.

At the end of Pershing Drive stood a gate shack that guarded the rear entrance of the base. I thought for sure Trace would left march us toward the post museum, to the dozens of World War II-era anti-aircraft guns on static display, each one crying out to be juvenile delinquished. But instead we veered right, where the chainlink fence dead-ended against an embankment. We followed the dirt road towards the base polo field, out where Ft. Bliss met I-10, where Army life ended and the civilian world began.

The field itself had not been used for many years, certainly not to the extent of its pre-World War I hey-day. Ft. Bliss had been a cavalry post then and distractions like polo were the next best thing to raiding Mexico. Stretched out along the far rim of the field loomed a forbidding berm of round, gray stones. The feature suggested flood control, but was probably meant to provide clear boundaries with what my parents liked to call "the outside."

The rain had chewed up the dirt road pretty good, and by the time we shambled over to the bleachers and condemned stable, our shoes were weighted with warm, shit-like mud the color of pottery.

Marvin kicked at the deep ruts that criss-crossed the area and appeared to circle the stable. "Somebody's been four-wheeling down here," he said, but no one responded. It was fairly well known that the place was a good spot for catching a buzz or drinking beer out of sight of underworked MP patrols.

Trace let his TDY bag slide off his back. He reached inside it with one hand and pulled out the grenade. He carefully clipped it to his jeans pocket, all the while purring into the cat's ear. Then he looked up at each of us, in turn, gauging our loyalty. His eyes looked buttery in the fading light. From somewhere deep in the interior of the base, a scratchy recording of a bugle sounded retreat.

"Intelligence," he said to us and paused, "radioed that this place is crawling with insurgents. They've sent us in to clear the way for the main body."

The rest of us looked at each other. A collective *Huh?* took one breath and died. On any other day, such ludicrous playacting would have met with ridicule, even for someone as threatening as Trace. But the grenade seemed to grant Trace great license, to be as serious or as utterly childish as he wanted to be.

Trace surveyed the scene and his eyes finally settled on the abandoned stable, its pitted stone walls ashen against the darkening sky. A low-slung roof overhung a pair of windows, forming the perfect brow of a skull perched upon two black sockets. We had gotten high within the structure many times in the past, climbing in through the windows, ignoring the padlocked wooden stable doors with their faded trespassing notice. Smattered about the foot of the doors lay several tufts of hay, ghostly traces of polo glories past.

"There's our objective," he said, his eyes pinched and intense. "Enemy bunker." He gestured with a nod toward the polo field, up past the rock wall and the freeway overpass beyond. "That's our line of retreat."

"Maybe we should let the cat go now," Danny said. "He's going to have a tough time finding his way home."

Trace stared back, then barked out of the side of his mouth: "Sergeant Woods!"

Marvin snapped the heels of his sneakers together and delivered an exaggerated salute. "Sir! Sergeant Woods reports as ordered!"

"We've got a soldier of questionable mettle here, Sergeant."

"Sir! Yes, sir! Shall I execute him, sir?!"

Trace shook his head. "We need every man for this mission. Even the cowards." He regarded me with a brief glance. "Even the brass."

Danny smiled stupidly. "I'm serious, man," he said, and reached out for the cat.

His hand never made it. "Ea-sy," Trace said, hissing each syllable through barred teeth as if readying to bite the oncoming fingers.

Danny dropped his hand and turned to me.

I averted my eyes. "It's getting dark," I said.

"The night is our ally," Trace said, and he backed away toward the stable.

"This isn't right," Danny said. His voice was threadbare and impotent. "We can't do this."

"He's just kidding," I said, even though, by now, I knew that he wasn't.

Trace had reverted to stealth mode, creeping up on the stable, careful to keep out of the window's line of sight. Then he turned and threw his back up against the wall just to the right of the window frame. The cat jolted as if from a deep sleep and stared out at us with an expression that seemed to say, "What in the hell is this guy—?" The cat's eyes never got the chance to finish relaying the sentiment. Trace grasped the animal around the midsection and swung it in a wide lazy arch. The dark window swallowed up the cat soundlessly.

Without pause, he plucked the grenade off his belt, bit down on the steel loop and yanked the explosive away from his mouth. A flick of the wrist and into the void went the grenade. He then spit out the pin, cupped his hands over his mouth and let loose with a wild cry of "FIRE IN THE HOLE!"

Marvin, Danny, and I watched in dreamlike stillness as our friend pushed off the wall and came charging toward us, a full-tilt blind sprint. Even after Trace shot past us, his mouth ballooning as though he were in a wind tunnel, we continued to stand there, dumbly frozen, unable or unwilling to believe the magnitude of what was coming.

The next few seconds are forever lost to me. I do know that my companions and I finally came to our senses because we suddenly found ourselves lying prone on the ground next to Trace, about thirty-odd yards from the stable. We were all looking wild-eyed at the structure, hearts pumping, breath panting, stomachs butterflying.

It was only when Trace raised his hand that we held our collective breath and were met with dead air silence, the quietest silence I have ever heard. Then, out of this nothing, came a faint gust of sound that did not fully register in my ears because it didn't fit at all with what I was seeing. It was the clear, undeniable sound of a horse's whinny followed by the sloppy flap of lips and the hiss of gigantic nostrils.

The explosion followed. We'll call it a succession of crashes, quick-marching in sublime order, all happening in the time it takes to blink. The thunderous blast, the shriek of metal and crack of wood, the shrapnel ricocheting off the stone walls. I've heard people say that gunfire sounds like firecrackers popping. But there was no mistaking the explosion. It sounded exactly like what it was—a grenade exploding—even though, outside of movies, I'd never heard one.

Of course, it wasn't the sound of the explosion that any of us thought about as our ears rang to the point of numbness, as we watched the teeming black smoke mushroom out of the stable windows. In fact, you could say that we were doing very little thinking at that moment. I'd even go so far as to say what happened next had me convinced I was an actor taking part in a movie. My mind even thought in script.

I turned to Marvin, knowing that he had the first line. As if cued from off set, he cried out, with Academy Award desperation: "Did . . . you . . . hear . . . *that*?"

It wasn't a question that wanted an answer. But we had to follow the script which is exactly what Trace did. "It was the cat," he said, hurriedly, as if trying to get his line out before . . . before . . .

Well, before the stable doors, now partially unhinged, were kicked apart and spilled to the ground like two huge playing cards. Out from the smoke strode a perfectly white horse, shimmering in its suddenness, its enormity. The beast hooved out about ten yards and rose up on its haunches. It nickered as it rose, its eyes as big as hard-boiled eggs stuck into its head. Its lips were pulled back over blackened gums and a single paint stroke of cardinal red blood glazed one muscular rump. Then the horse clapped its front hooves together as though in grand appreciation of what we had done.

And I can tell you this: I can tell you that all that was needed at that precise moment was a movie director—complete with a bull horn, beret, and saddle pants—to stride forward toward the edge of the smoke and yell, "Cut! It's a Wrap! Print it!" Or whatever it is they yell.

That was all that was needed, but like every catastrophic blunder since the dawn of man, all that was needed was the only goddamned thing missing.

I hadn't been completely honest with Trace and the others. First off, I had no intention of enlisting in the Army despite my blood oath to the contrary. I had yet to determine how to explain it to them in a way they'd understand, in a way that would allow us to keep our friendship. Trace, for one, would bludgeon me with told-you-so's. In a way, this didn't matter to me, but in another, it was all that mattered. Life often boils down to choosing what group of people you'd rather betray. Parents are the easiest—they forgive. Peers don't follow that rule. They never forgive. It's built into the whole friendship system. And when you've got a guy like Trace hammering home the details, you can forget about walking away without feeling like you've sold your best buddy out to the POW camp commandant for a slice of bread.

Complicating my choice was the unbelievable fact that, at seventeen, I wanted to be just like my father. He had the nerve to recognize it and had set me up pretty with a ROTC recruiter at Syracuse, an old army buddy of his from Vietnam. The first step, my dad said. From there, I could transfer to Officer Training School. It wasn't West Point, but it could get the Army to pay for medical training and more.

None of this would make sense to the guys. Not even if I described to them the moment of truth, the turning point that clarified my future. The day my father came home with blood on his whites. There had been an accident on the base firing range. A backfired mortar shell killed a couple of soldiers and left several more fighting for their lives. The survivors were dumped into my father's lap, a major then, in charge of the post emergency room. I remember when he came home that night. I stood with my mother at the door of the laundry room, a textbook in my hand, watching my dad wearily strip off his bloody clothes. He stopped my mother from putting them in the washing machine, saying to her, "No, you can't save them."

I remember smiling proudly, feeling the text book—with its unfinished assignment which, until that moment, had caused me nothing but frustration—and I knew then that I had to be like him. Not so much for the officer status, but because I had to have a job where I could save a life and still show traces afterwards. I had to have a job where my clothes couldn't be saved. Explain that to a guy like Trace and he'd laugh in your face, call you a traitor and what's worse—you'd feel like one.

Of course, all this came at a point before I made my ultimate break with adolescence, with childish things. All this came before the grenade, before I stood with my Ft. Bliss friends at dusk in the mud of the polo field, watching Reveille, Omar Bradley's favorite parade horse, emerge from the curtain of smoke and into our midst like the butcher bringing the bill.

We backed away from the animal, which responded by clopping eagerly toward us, huffing and sneezing, a spirited and stretched look of pain in its wide eyes. I can say now in hindsight that it terrified me. I was simply unable to come to grips with its bizarre, yet understandable behavior. I even found myself recalling that old story about when American Indians first set eyes on European horses and thought they were giant dogs. I sympathized.

Out of this fantastic confusion came the wail of a siren. It was then that we took our first steps back to reality. It was then that our minds began working clearly and precisely. It was then that we knew exactly what we were up against and, with the rich blue blood of the sons of warriors, we knew exactly what to do.

We ran.

I'd say we went backwards at first, spinning awkwardly, stumbling toward full steam, our sneakers cutting into the soft wet grass with determination. As I picked up speed, I threw a glance over each shoulder, processing information that went from bad to worse, jumbled in my dire need to outrun what I was seeing. Over my left shoulder, the smoky stable looked awash with destruction and embarrassment. Braced along its side—the side formerly hidden from our view—the last sliver of sunlight glinted off the metal of what was clearly a horse trailer, its pintle hook jacked up on blocks. I would have bet my future, which was already on the line, that it had not been there only the day before.

Over my right shoulder I caught a glimpse of the road leading into the field. The source of the siren was a MP jeep racing to the scene, fishtailing in the mud, going too fast for its own good. We would find out later that base headquarters had placed the horse in the stable temporarily, until a larger facility on the post proper could be prepared. The two MPs left to guard the animal, failing to see the honor of their assignment, locked the gate and took their jeep up to Burger King out on Sheridan Road for a quick bite. They would testify that they'd been gone only twenty minutes, exactly the time we'd wandered down to the field.

Of course, at the time, we were blissfully ignorant of anything except what lay directly to our front. The rocky berm that rimmed the field.

In what felt like three gigantic steps, I found myself mud-caked and out of breath but coming upon the base of the berm. Without a thought to slowing down, I leapt onto the rocky hill. I dug my toes into the softball-sized stones and clawed with my hands for balance and extra push. I could hear my friends scrambling after me, cursing at the rockslide I left in my wake. Someone—I think it was Marvin—yelled, "Holy shit, it's coming after us!"

"Keep climbing!" I yelled, pulling myself up and over the summit. "They'll never get the Jeep over the rocks!"

"Not the Jeep! The mother-fucking horse!"

Teetering at the top of the berm, I swung around and beheld the immensity of the polo field. Our problem wasn't the Jeep which was making slow progress down the muddy path and hadn't even reached the stable yet. Our problem was the giant white horse which was trotting after us at a half gallop, mud clinging to its legs like socks, a shaft of wood protruding from its hip and quivering like a small diving board. The animal paused at the base of the rocks and delivered a robust snort.

"Move it!" I shouted at my companions who had paused mid-way up the rocks to gawk at our pursuer. "Keep climbing! He won't get up these rocks. There's no way—"

To my amazement and slight embarrassment, the white horse began its ascent, clopping and crab stepping up the rocks.

"I'm not seeing this," I said to no one.

"That's what they do," Danny said as he reached me, wheezing for air. "It thinks it's in a show."

Trace came right behind him, stammering, "We need to—We need to—"

I didn't wait for a complete sentence. I snatched Danny's arm and Trace's shirt, and we all nearly tumbled down the opposite embankment. With our path marked by the freeway lights above, we tromped across a utility road, over the railroad trestle and into the cavernous darkness beneath the highway overpass. The horse followed, its hindquarters sashaying with all the grace of a couple of clowns dressed up in a horse suit.

The four of us reached the base of one great pillar, and paused there to catch our breath. We stood in a semi-circle, hidden by the shadows. The horse had since slowed its pursuit and now walked calmly over to us, joining our small huddle. It shook its long, maned neck and puffed. Just one of the gang.

I searched the faces of my companions, including the horse, and was struck by how similar their eyes looked. Wide and dumb, like a boatload of clubbed fish. There, in the darkness, I had a tough time telling which eyes were human and which were equine. I had no trouble telling how desperate they were for leadership and direction. Plenty.

So I managed to raise one hand and point a finger toward the pair of eyes I assumed belonged to Marvin. With the strong voice that belied my own confusion at our predicament, I ordered him to go back over the hill, to keep a look out, to tell us if anyone— anyone human—was following us. He stared back at me as though I'd just asked him to throw his body onto a live grenade for the good of the squad. But after an encouraging snort from the horse, Marvin complied.

I then took quick stock of our surroundings, my eyes adjusting to the darkness. Trace was leaning up against the pillar, struggling to breathe. Graffiti took shape on the concrete walls and braces around him. The swish of cars overhead, like surf breaking on a beach, had a strangely calm effect. That is, until the distant sirens began to multiply, undulating through the night air.

"What about this?" Danny finally said, half-gesturing to the horse, as if he didn't want to offend it.

"First things first," I said, but only because it sounded good. I didn't have the faintest clue as to what constituted the "first thing."

Danny licked his lips, then reached toward the backside of the animal. He tried to get hold of the wood sliver, presumably to remove it. The horse responded by sidestepping away from him. Danny reached again, and he and the horse came full circle, a comical dance that would have gone on forever if I hadn't yelled at him to stop.

"Why?" he said.

"*Why*? Because you didn't wash your hands first, how's that?"

"God," Trace groaned. I turned to him, waiting for something more than this reflexive sigh. His presence seemed all the more glaring because of his silence. I stepped forward and put my hand on his shoulder. His shirt was damp with sweat. "You okay?" I said.

He looked accusingly at me, and said, "What the hell's that supposed to mean?"

I paused, recognizing a plump anger in his voice. "What else could it mean?" I said, then repeated slowly, "Are . . . you . . . oh-kay?"

He swept my hand from his shoulder and took a step toward me. "Why didn't somebody tell me? Huh?" A glimmer of light reflected in his tight, gray eyes. He looked ready to massacre a village of women and children.

"Nobody knew," I said.

He spat into shadows and shouted, with intense derision, "Hah! Nobody knew!" He pointed at the horse. "Nobody *knew*?!"

The horse whinnied again, more in agreement than denial.

We all tensed as Marvin came scrambling through the faint light towards us.

"Anything?" Danny said.

Marvin huffed and struggled to swallow. "Nah, man, they called it a night, packed up, and went home. Jesus, what the hell do you think? They're gearing up to hunt us down like . . . like . . . goddamn terrorists!"

"We are terrorists," I said.

"Did you see Pontoon?" Danny said to Marvin.

"Did I see *what?*"

"The cat. Did he make it?"

Overhead and out of sight, a helicopter spirited through the night air. We each ducked as though it could have clipped our heads off.

"Now we're fucked," Danny said.

"As opposed to when?" I said.

Marvin was close to tears. He started to rock back and forth, groaning like a woman in labor. "This is some shit, man," he said. "This is some sticky ass shit."

"Okay, okay," I said, making calming gestures with my hands. "Nobody's dead. Be thankful for that."

"It would have been better," Trace said, distantly. "It would have been better if somebody was dead."

"Well, nobody is. We'll have to settle for that."

He fixed his eyes on me again. They burned with past, present and future grievances. "You being funny with me, Cadet?"

"Trace, I don't think I could dream up a worse time to be funny with you."

But that wasn't about to satisfy him. I could see his fists tightening and untightening. His neck muscles stiffened and his teeth ground. The time of our confrontation, at least in his mind, was finally at hand.

And we would certainly have fought, right then and there, except that Danny and Marvin beat us to it.

"Somebody *is* dead," Danny said angrily, demanding recognition. He looked at each of us, even the horse, then said, "Pontoon. Pontoon is dead."

And that's when Marvin shoved Danny back against the pillar and spit out, "Quit whining about the cat!"

"Oh sure. It's just a cat, right? A cat that was minding its own business!"

"What, was your mom gonna cook it for dinner or something!"

"Koreans eat dogs, you dumb ass! You can't even insult me right!"

"But I can kick your commie ass!" He pulled Danny toward him, seizing his head in a deathlock. Danny squirmed free and began flailing his arms, striking only air. Trace and I stared at each other, resentfully, ridiculously. The horse took its cue from the commotion and rose up on its hindlegs, clapping its hooves again.

Danny and Marvin fell to the ground in a dark knot of anger, their bodies kicking the greasy rail gravel in all directions. I yelled at Trace to help me separate the two. To my surprise, he did what I yelled.

When we pulled the two of them to their feet, they stood there, heads hanging, glancing sideways as if looking for a quick and easy punch. I shouted at them that we didn't have time for this shit and that we had to split up, to take our chances getting back to the base.

I told each of them where to go. Marvin would take the tracks west, I said, I would take them east. Danny would head north into the city and catch a bus back to the south gate. Trace would head into the suburbs and follow the freeway that looped around to the other side of the base.

Danny, wiping blood from the corner of his mouth, gestured to the horse and said, "What about—"

"Don't say it!" I shouted back.

He didn't.

"I'm taking the tracks east," Trace said, once again squaring off on me, daring me to challenge him. "You do what you want, but I'm taking the—"

"So do it!" I shouted back into his face. "Quit crying and *do* it!"

We all turned and started off, splintering away to our own destinies. Marvin trudged to the west along the rail ties, Danny vanished into the darkness of the overpass, I scaled the concrete ramp toward I-10. As I fought the incline, my muddy sneakers grudgingly finding purchase, I shot a glance back over my shoulder even though I had a strong feeling I would regret it.

In the dark bruise of shadows, I glimpsed Trace jogging awkwardly, hands jammed in his pockets, lurching along the ties. Following close behind was the horse. It had picked him out of our little line-up. It had claimed him. And despite the unfairness of it—which is to say, the poetic justice of it—regret was the least of my emotions.

Trace never lost the horse. The MPs found it the next day, parked outside his drab little house, munching on the overgrown shrubbery. Trace was arrested, taken to security headquarters, then released to his father who promptly squirreled him away while they waited for the half-ass plea agreement to pan out. Meanwhile, the parade went on as usual—the horse, bandaged and drugged, played its part with none the wiser. Every day I expected to get a knock on the door, but none came. Marvin, Danny, and I avoided one another. You would have thought we were strangers.

After about week, Marvin finally contacted me by phone and passed on the inside scoop. His date of enlistment was fast approaching and he seemed to want to purge the affair from his mind before he signed away the next four years. He had called Trace from the Shoppette payphone ("just in case the lines were tapped") and was lucky to have Trace answer. Trace had tried his best to lose the horse. He had trekked along several miles of tracks, went through every alley he came across, even crisscrossed a stream, but the horse tracked him with a purpose. At dawn, Trace finally relented and snuck onto base, entered his house, then lay on his bed in the hope that the horse would just go away on its own. Of course, it didn't. And when his father burst into his room demanding to know just what the hell was going on, Trace had, according to Marvin, responded: "What horse?"

"*What horse?*'" Marvin repeated to me, sourly, as if he had suddenly lost total faith in his lifelong religion. "His old man didn't even mention a horse and Trace says, *'What horse?'* Do you hear what I'm saying, man?"

"I get it," I assured him. "I guess Trace must have lost his old-fashioned horse sense with all that running around."

"You shouldn't laugh," Marvin said. "He's pretty pissed off."

I grew silent. "You think he'll turn us in?"

"If we're lucky," Marvin answered, then abruptly ended the call.

There followed a period of lazy time, a month or so where everyday seemed to be the same and nothing ever happened. Only the whine of cicadas and helicopters on maneuvers, all sandwiched between two strained bugle recordings of reveille and retreat. One morning—I couldn't tell you which—I awoke with the confidence that no one was ever coming. Even so, the absence of Trace made him all the more present in my thoughts.

I think it was just after I informed my father that I'd be joining the ROTC program at Syracuse that I saw Trace again. I was standing near the hot dog stand, outside the P/X. I hardly recognized him as he strutted up. He was wearing a jean jacket that stood out grotesquely in the noon sun. His head was cropped close and haggard, as though he'd fought the person cutting his hair. It was the kind of institutional hair cut you'd expect to see in an attempt to get rid of lice. I felt no pity for him whatsoever and wondered, guiltily, if we had ever really been friends.

He drew up close, looked around, then poked his chin at me.

I nodded back. I was about to ask him how he was, but he cut me off. "They wanted to know who was with me," he said. "They wanted to know real bad, but I kept it in." He tapped his chest with his knuckles to show where he had kept it. "I kept it in like you never saw."

"I appreciate it."

"You shouldn't. It wasn't a favor." He shrugged to show that none of it mattered. Then he leaned forward, and eased out of his jacket pocket the butt of a revolver—just a glimpse. "This," he said conspiratorially, "is for the one who narked on me. The one who narked is getting a little present for his birthday. Or Christmas. Whatever comes first."

I swallowed and looked around, trying to appear nonchalant. "What makes you think somebody narked?"

He laughed dryly. "I have my sources."

I told him that I had heard the MPs found the horse outside his house and he responded by shaking his head with immense confidence. "Didn't prove anything. Not a goddamn thing. Those MP clowns couldn't find their own heads if their hands were glued to their ears." He spit between his feet, into the gutter. "Somebody narked."

"You're nuts." I said it without malice, a simple statement of fact of which even he had to be aware. I wondered if I would have said it a month ago, before the grenade rolled into our lives, before the grenade cemented—rather than blew apart—my dreams of what I would become.

He nodded as if I had said something predictable. "Am I?" he said. "That's what my recruiter said. He won't touch me with a ten-foot pole now. You'd think they'd want people like us enlisting in the Army!"

I looked away, but felt him watching me. He sighed, almost sympathetically, and whispered, "I guess you'll be going for that commission now, eh?" His tone only served to make his voice all the louder. I waited for him to say something else, something bitter, derisive.

Instead, he said, "Danny."

"What?"

"Danny. He's the one. I always knew he'd fold. Well now he's going to get the surprise of his life. He ain't gonna see it coming, but he's getting it. He's getting it like his precious cat got it. . . ."

"It wasn't him," I said.

"What makes you so sure?"

"He's too worried about his own neck."

"Well he better start worrying for real now." He patted his coat pocket, then stepped off the curb.

I could have easily said my goodbyes, let him walk out of my life. Hell, I couldn't wait to never see him again. But something stopped me. Something made me say, "I did it." Clear, stark, challenging.

Trace shoved his hand into the pocket with the gun, a reflexive action. His face stared back at me, shining with hatred, defeat. He spit again.

Finally, with a sudden quizzical look in his eyes, as if he just recalled a forgotten appointment, he turned away and strode off across the parking lot. I can't tell you what it was that made him back down, but I know it wouldn't have happened before the grenade.

As I headed for home, I thought of Danny and quickly changed direction, hurrying to his house. I wondered if Trace would beat me there.

Danny sat on the front stoop of his duplex and didn't seem at all surprised to see me even though we hadn't spoken in a month. He was sweating and disheveled from unfinished yard work. He was also cradling something in his arms.

I was about to ask him if he'd seen Trace around when I noticed what it was he was holding.

"Jesus, is that. . . ?"

Danny nodded. "My neighbor's cat." He stroked the animal, which responded by playfully swatting at his hand.

"So the lucky bastard made it," I said.

"You think so?" He propped the cat up on the edge of his lap and said, with a slight irritation, "Talk to it."

"Talk to it?"

"Go on. Say something to it."

"To the cat? What do you mean? Say what?"

"Anything. Go on."

I shrugged. "Meow."

"Notice its reaction?"

"Are you stoned, man?"

"There is none. It didn't hear you. It's deaf."

"Look, I just came over to see if you wanted to catch a flick or something," I said, making it up on the spot.

"How is it supposed to survive in the wild if it can't hear?"

I shrugged again. "You want to catch a flick or not?"

"I'm serious. We've got a responsibility here."

"Goodbye."

I turned and walked away. And I don't think I've ever felt as lonely as I did at that moment, as if I were experiencing exactly what Trace experienced as he walked away from me just a short time before. And I might have felt like that forever, I think, except that Danny yelled after me, yelled for me to stop, to wait up. That he was coming with me.

ROAR

Clay Hamilton stood where he always stood at dusk—every dusk, it seemed to him, for the last ten years—staring into the open freezer door of a gas station mini-mart, the present establishment known improbably as *Big Bart's Belly Barn*. The cold air stuck to his face like paint. He kept still for several seconds, testing all internal alarms for watchful eyes, then thrust his hand forward and snatched up a handful of frozen burritos. In the time it would take to flinch, they were jammed into his inside jacket pocket, making friendly with a nine millimeter automatic, a pen light, and the beer he'd stolen moments before. A casual observer would have suspected nothing.

He glanced up at the fisheye mirror wedged into a corner ceiling, above a rack of Wonder Bread. The attendant, a teenager with his head shaved smooth above the ears, was sitting on a stool reading a textbook. When Clay came in, the kid had given him the once over, but quickly dismissed any notion that he was a threat. With a balding head, creased slacks and quiet loafers, Clay probably reminded the teenager of someone familiar, a camp counselor or the principal at his high school. Principals and counselors weren't a threat. They didn't rob or steal. At least, not burritos.

When Clay rapped his knuckles on the counter, the attendant rose off the stool slowly, eyes still locked on a line of text. Clay laid a crumpled ten-dollar bill—the last of his hard currency—between them.

"Just the gas then?" the attendant said.

Clay nodded and gestured toward the freezer doors. "Not much of a selection back there."

The attendant shrugged. He stabbed a button on the cash register, which dinged and sprang open. "Can't please everyone," he said.

Clay smiled. "Story of my life."

He stepped back out into the dry Texas night and slid into the driver's seat of his battered, but juiced-up '92 Olds Cutlass. He handed a burrito to Ellie beside him, then tossed one into the back seat, into Lem's fat lap.

Clay cracked his beer and chugged. The attendant was watching him from the brightly lit store, perhaps wondering for the first time why Clay needed a jacket on such a warm night. Clay waved as he pulled away. Mechanically, as though still suspicious but also well conditioned against rudeness, the attendant waved back.

"I don't get it," Lem said. "What am I supposed to do with this?" He was holding the burrito close to his face as if trying to read the ingredients.

Clay could make out the dark round shape of Lem's head in the rearview mirror. The teenager's eyes looked like two glassy slits in the dashboard lights. "You said you were starving," Clay said.

"But this is frozen."

"Did you want me to heat it up before I stole it?"

"Couldn't you get something that didn't need to be cooked?"

"Stop bitching, Lem," Ellie said. "It won't kill you."

"But it's frozen. Feel it."

Lem held the burrito near Ellie's face and she pushed his hand away. "I have my own," she said. She reached out and began massaging the taut muscles at the back of Clay's neck, something she did whenever she anticipated he might strangle her brother. "How much farther, babe?"

"Couple hours."

"You hear that, Lem. Two more hours and we'll be rich."

Lem was chewing methodically. "There's ice in this thing. I'm eating ice."

Clay wielded the bulky car onto the two-laned highway and headed south. The dark desert hummed by in silence. There was a strong wind pushing over the road, and the steering wheel shook in Clay's grip. The air through his open window took on a sugared, gritty taste. He kept just under the speed limit, knowing that for the cops who prowled these stretches, "moving violation" was just another word for "Christmas bonus."

Even at radar jamming speed, they reached the outskirts of Silver Lake in just half an hour. Clay was thankful that Ellie didn't mention his miscalculation. It would have only brought them bad luck. And if there was ever a scam that needed luck—good luck and quick fingers—this was the one.

On the phone the night before, his grandfather had sounded drugged with age, boredom or both. He also sounded eager and relieved. "Fine, great, never better," he said without suspicion, when Clay asked him how he had been over the last ten years. "Army? Don't say," he said, when Clay explained how *he* had been. In the background, Clay's grandmother kept saying, "Who is it who is it who is it . . ." until her words ran together like static. Clay could see her tugging on his grandfather's sleeve like a small child. Still, the old man didn't allow a hint of irritation to disrupt his eager tone, and when Clay explained that he was coming for a visit, his grandfather simply said, "Fine. You know us. We ain't going nowhere."

Going nowhere would have been the perfect motto for Silver Lake, the town Clay had called home from the time his mother succumbed to a drug overdose to his self-extraction from high school—a tally of three years. Now, driving along the deserted main street, its diagonal parking spaces clogged with neglected tractors and farming equipment, a far more appropriate slogan came to mind: *Gone.*

The town square consisted of one small tavern, a grocery store, the "Silver Lake Municipal Center" in need of repairs, and a cluster of other buildings that looked strip-searched and gutted in the streetlights. The church where Clay had received his last communion straddled one corner, its parking lot almost as large as the square itself. A lone traffic light blinked yellow at the main intersection.

Clay turned onto a side street that sloped down and away from the square. The street was lined with squat homes set off by high fences and dying trees. He drove until the road dead-ended against a shapeless desert, parked across from the last house on the street, then cut the engine. The dead motor ticked like a clock.

"Nice," Lem said. "So what do you have to be to live around here? Besides paroled."

"It wasn't always like this," Clay said. His eyes searched the house and its surroundings for any sign of life or movement.

"If this guy's so rich," Lem said, "what's he doing in a dump like this?"

Ellie twisted around and stuck her finger at her brother. "Are you getting stupid again?"

"What did I say?"

"Keep mouthing off and see what happens. See how fast you're all by yourself. Clay's not gonna need any convincing."

Lem smiled and glanced at Clay. He said, "Clay wouldn't do me no harm. He's a teddy bear. That's his biggest problem."

Ellie eased back in her seat. "What's wrong?" she said to Clay.

Clay shrugged and tipped his head toward the dark house. "The old man's truck is gone."

"Is that bad?"

"I don't know. He never leaves the house at night. Never. He's got bad eyes."

"It's better if he's not here."

Clay shook his head. "He's got the keys. I can't get into his footlocker without the keys."

"Let's just take the footlocker," Lem suggested.

Clay ignored him and spoke more to himself than his companions. "Why would he leave? He knows we're coming."

"Could your mom have taken the truck?" Ellie said.

"My mother's dead," Clay said.

"Your grandmother then. Whoever."

"Gretta doesn't drive. She doesn't do anything that requires sanity. Or balance."

Ellie marked her impatience by dragging her fingernails up the side stitching of her jeans. "We'll go in and wait then," she said.

Clay didn't answer for some time. Finally, he nodded, reached into his jacket for the nine millimeter, and slipped the weapon down under his seat. Then he swiveled to face them fully. "Ok, no slip ups now," he said. "Ellie and I got married six months ago. I'm a supervisor at Ricoh Tech in Arkansas, making good money. Lem here is your brother."

"I am her brother," Lem said.

Clay pointed at Ellie. "Don't forget. You're pregnant." He looked her over in the dark. "Three months, we'll say."

"Try again," she said.

"Okay, two."

Ellie groaned suddenly, then doubled over, clutching her stomach.

"What?"

"I just felt the baby kick."

Lem's fat body quaked with laughter and he drummed the back of the seat until Clay told him to shut the fuck up. Clay stared across at Ellie. "Please get serious," he said. "I've been wait-ing a long time for this one. What's the matter now?"

"Nothing," Ellie said. "We should have stopped somewhere. It would be easier for me to lie about being married if we actually got married."

"That doesn't make any sense."

"Makes perfect sense. We love each other."

"I mean your sentence doesn't make any sense."

"Like I said, it's clear to me."

"Jesus please us," Lem said, slapping the head rests. "Are we doing this or what?"

When Clay knocked on the front door, Gretta Hamilton peeked through the curtain at the kitchen window, disappeared for a full minute, then finally reappeared at the door, cracking it open an inch, enough to peer out with one eye. She was a small woman and had to look up at them.

Once she recognized her grandson, she stepped outside with-out hesitation and clutched him fanatically, slipping her thin arms around his waist and squeezing. Clay did not return the hug. His limp body swayed in her embrace.

"What a grand surprise!" she said, her eyes glistening in the porch light. "Of all of the people on all of the earth. We were just talking about you, honeybunch. Just tonight, we were talking about you."

"Clay, Gretta." He gently took hold of her wrists and eased himself out of her grip. "My name is Clay. Still."

"Of course it is." She smiled, showing off a tiny row of teeth much too white to be real. "Clay Patrick Hamilton." Her wide-eyed expression swept from Clay to Ellie to Lem and kept on going, off into the night, as though she couldn't quite recover from the momentum. Clay pushed past her into the house, followed by Ellie and Lem. Gretta reached across the threshold after them and clasped the doorknob. For a moment, Clay thought she might actually close the door on herself, but she finally hitched forward, using the knob like a cane.

Her complexion looked strained, propped and powdered by a thick layer of make-up. She wore a full-length apron with a caption across the front that read, *Don't ask me, I Just Cook Here!*

"You should have called, honeybunch," she said, out of breath. "I would have made something."

"I did call."

"You did?"

"Last night."

She pondered this seriously, inserting a finger into her springy gray hair and scratching her head. "There was a call indeed," she said.

"Boy, something sure smells good," Lem said.

Gretta clapped her hands together and said brightly, "You're just in time. We're having guests."

"Cool," Lem said.

"What's the occasion?" Ellie said.

"My grandson is coming home! After ten years, he's finally coming home. And he's bringing his new wife!"

"How nice," Ellie said. She looked at Clay.

Clay shook his head. He strode into the living room, taking a quick but mindful survey. The small room was—as it had always been—over-crowded with furniture, each piece representing its own design scheme and primary color. Two couches—one too many—absorbed most of the space and were set up in an L-shape around a coffee table fashioned out of a tree stump. Affixed to one wall was an artificial fireplace, complete with an artificial log and artificial fire.

Fanning outward from the mantle and blocking the opening into the dining room was a small forest of ceramic animals— elephants rearing up, their snouts balancing dusty trays; obedient lap dogs of all breeds; several lions, most set back on their haunches in regal poses. Nearly all the sculptures were over two feet high, big enough to be a tripping hazard as well as unsightly. Beyond this display was a long table bedecked with steaming plates of finger food. The plates were arranged carefully around a centerpiece that reminded Clay of an abandoned bird's nest. The tart odor of barbecue sauce hung in the air.

Clay took a seat on the couch, planting a foot on the coffee table, and motioned for Ellie to sit down beside him. Gretta perched on the edge of the other couch, her fingers nervously tugging at the hem of her apron. She cocked her head to one side and stared dreamily at Clay. "Still the same baby face," she said with airy pride, her voice just above a whisper. She turned to Ellie. "A judge brought him to us one day, you know. They told us he'd be nothing but trouble. They told us he couldn't be saved. But I took one look at that baby face and knew they were wrong."

Clay yawned. "Where's Howard?" he said.

"Who?"

"Your husband. Where is he?"

As though snapping awake, Gretta launched into an enthusiastic explanation about his grandfather's new-found love of the road. "Ever since he got his special glasses," she concluded, "he just drives and drives and drives. All over the place. Especially at night. Making up for all the years he couldn't."

"All the years nurturing the family's mental health," Clay mumbled.

"What's that, honeybunch?"

"Nothing."

Lem was standing amidst the maze of ceramic animals. He had made an attempt to walk through them and now seemed to be trapped. He backed up, stopped, then turned completely around before stopping again. He kept glancing at the food on the table, his obvious destination.

"These are really great," Lem said helplessly when he noticed the three of them watching him.

"I made them myself," Gretta said. "I'm not allowed to have real pets."

With a combination of side-steps and forward shuffles, Lem finally disentangled himself from the statues. He stopped beside a ceramic lion, although his eyes never left the table. "Wow, this one's close to looking real," he said, then reached down and patted the head of the lion, pointlessly.

"Its eyes glow at night," Gretta said, beaming. "But don't expect it to roar."

"I won't," Lem said.

"They must have taken a long time to make," Ellie said.

"Oh, days and days," Gretta said, her arms waving dramatically.

"She didn't make them," Clay said. He yawned again and glanced at his watch. "She buys them from those stands near gas stations."

"I do?" Gretta said.

"Man, what a set up," Lem said. He had turned fully upon the table, his arms spread apart in surprise as though he had only just discovered the bounty. He angled his rotund frame in an effort to best survey the food. His nostrils flared.

"Not too close now," Gretta cautioned him. "Everything's laid out just perfect."

"Don't worry," Lem said, turning to wink at her. "I won't eat *every*thing." Using his thick thumb and forefinger like a pincer, Lem reached for an oval plate laden with toothpick-impaled weenies.

Gretta reacted by springing to her feet and dashing across the floor toward him. She navigated the ceramic animals in three deft steps, cocked her arm skyward, and swatted the back of his hand with enough force to leave an immediate red mark. The weenie was dislodged from the toothpick and fell to the floor, bouncing around like a tiny rubber football before disappearing under the table.

"Hey!" Lem yelled, his mouth opening and closing as if still trying to taste the weenie it was promised.

Gretta harrumphed angrily at him, her hands fumbling into her front apron pocket. She pulled out a small plastic water pistol and began squirting Lem in the face and eyes, driving him backward. "Hey, c'mon, lady!" he said. "C'mon, don't!"

Ellie turned to Clay, her expression shocked and pleading.

Clay could only smile. Finally, he said, "Have a seat, Lem."

Lem retreated as fast as his weight would allow him, finally falling into an overstuffed club chair pressed against the wall. His face and shirt collar were dripping wet. The red mark on his hand stood out like rouge.

Gretta, satisfied with her defense of the table, backed into the living room, both hands still gripping the water pistol. She glanced sideways at Lem as though he might leap up and make another run for the food.

Outside, a long wailing sound echoed through the night. It started low and mournful and rose to a sharp, wavering screech.

"Good God," Ellie said. "Is that a siren?"

Gretta leaned toward her and whispered conspiratorially. "It's one of the lions. Not these little ones. *Real* lions." She looked away, her eyes moving around the room as though following the sound. "They're all over the place. They've eaten all the neighbors."

Clay let out another sigh and stood up. He walked past Gretta, over to the sliding glass door. "Kid next door," he explained, peering out. "I remember when his parents bought him that electric guitar. Sounds like they never invested in lessons."

Through the glass door, Clay could see the far end of the neighbor's backyard, grassless and dull in the moonlight. Dark, broken farm machinery sat heaped along the fence. Scattered across the yard were stretches of chains to mark where family pets had once died of thirst.

Without turning, Clay said, "Honey, why don't you help Gretta in the kitchen. I bet there's still lots to do."

Gretta clapped her hands together and said, "Yes, yes, yes. Hundreds of things to do. And not much time left. My grandson will be here soon." Ellie rose stiffly, a tired smile pressed onto her face. She followed Gretta into the kitchen.

When the two women were gone, Lem stood up. He pulled at the sleeve of his T-shirt, wiping his face with it. "Did you see what she did, man?" he said. "Did you see that loony bullshit?"

"We usually wait until she goes to sleep before we eat anything."

Lem smacked his fist into his palm. "One more squirt and I would have put her out of her misery."

"You wouldn't have done anything except get wetter, so shut up."

"She's lucky, that's all I'm saying."

Clay walked across the room to the front door. He looked out through the curtain, then returned to the living room, his eyes roving around with calm urgency.

"Is this our boy?" Lem said. He was holding one of the many pictures lining the mantle. The photo depicted a squat, bald man standing in front of a store. The sign over the door read, *Silver Lake Pawn*. Beneath this was an even smaller sign that read, *We Buy, We Sell, We Habla Espanol!* Lem grinned. "Yikes. Now I know where your good looks come from."

Clay wasn't listening. He had slipped open a drawer to a rickety lamp table and began pushing through the nest of letters and receipts stuffed inside.

"That's what I'm talking about," Lem said. "Screw the deviled eggs, right?" In a moment, he was rifling through a small jewelry box that sat atop the mantle. He quickly came up with a battered wrist watch, one band broken off. He felt the weight of it in his hand, then jammed it into his pocket. Clay was at his side immediately, snatching his wrist with both hands. "Put it back," Clay said.

"Let go!"

"Guess you didn't hear me." Clay grasped the teen's shoulder now, pushing him against the fake brick face of the fireplace. He twisted Lem's arm back over his flabby mid-section.

"Owww!" Lem cried. "Okay, man, *okay!*" With a huff, he dug out the watch and tossed it back into the box.

Clay held a finger up in front of Lem's face. "You keep your fat paws off everything," he said. "There's a grocery store up the street. You feel like stealing, go steal yourself some Twinkies."

"Look, I didn't come here to baby-sit some loony bitch—"

Clay delivered a short jab into Lem's chest, his knuckles thudding against bone. Lem staggered backward and coughed. "Next time," Clay said, "I plant one in your face, okay?"

Lem rubbed his chest. He looked like he might cry, but then began surveying himself angrily, as if to take detailed stock of his new injuries for some future legal action.

Clay returned to the open table drawer, this time reaching deep inside. With great care, he produced an oil-black .38 revolver. He unhinged the chamber in a calm, workmanlike motion, and shook out a handful of bullets which he deposited into his jeans pocket. Then he snapped the chamber back into place and returned the weapon to the drawer.

Turning, he found Lem glaring at him, eyes still burning with pain. "Some jacked up family you got there, man," the teenager said. "My sister really hit the jackpot."

Clay blew him a kiss, then ascended the stairs to the second floor. He made his way down the dark hall, not bothering to even glance into the open doorway of his old bedroom. Instead, he went straight into his grandparents' room at the end of the corridor.

With the penlight stuck in his mouth like a cigar, he pushed aside the heavy clothing in the closet and reached down into the corner, his hand feeling around by memory. There, wedged against the wall, surrounded by clumps of shoes, he saw an army-issue footlocker. A blocky padlock held the lid in place. Beside the footlocker stood a .22 caliber rifle, but Clay left it alone.

Just then, headlights washed across the front window, and he heard the grate of tires rolling up the driveway. Clay hurried back downstairs. His mouth was already open and prepared to tell Lem to get ready, but the living room was empty. It took Clay only a moment to see that the sliding glass door at the back was ajar.

"Fat brat," he muttered, hurrying over. He flicked on the backyard light, looked around, but saw no one. He called out Lem's name. The only sound that answered him was the hacking drone of a tortured guitar next door and the front door jostling open.

"And there he is," was what Clay's grandfather had to say. He stood just inside the front doorway, stomping hard on the mat as though he were shaking snow from his boots. Gretta and Ellie emerged from the kitchen.

The old man looked as sick as he had sounded on the phone. His eyes were wet and obscured behind a pair of see-the-future glasses and his clothes hung disarranged over a sad, rawboned frame. He was so thin that the skin on his face and hands looked ready to shred apart, like rice paper. The cold ivory of his bones showed through. As he appraised Clay, he didn't appear to believe what he was seeing. His mouth opened to make some further statement, one that was wise and ultimate, but promptly closed up, perhaps worried that what he was seeing might disappear. One scrawny hand gripped a compact ring of keys that hung heavy at his side.

Clay moved forward cautiously and offered a handshake. His grandfather looked down at the outstretched hand, a confused expression coming over his face as though he were expected to eat it. After an awkward moment, he clasped the hand, pulling Clay toward him, embracing the whole of his grandson's body. Clay patted the old man's back. When the two finally parted, everyone looked politely away.

"Howard," the old man told Ellie when Clay introduced her. "Call me Howard."

His eyes narrowed as he seemed to think better of it. "Or Grandpa. Hell, Grandpa's fine, too."

"Okay," she said and shrugged. "Grandpa."

Howard visibly relaxed and stepped back into the open doorway, looking her over. "Clay said last night you were expecting."

"Yes, I know I don't look—"

"Five months?"

Ellie managed a strained smile. "Two," she said.

Howard looked at Clay, then back to Ellie. "Say, I didn't mean . . ."

"No, no, it's alright."

"Jeez, you know, because I wouldn't know a pregnant woman from . . . from . . ."

Gretta tugged on Howard's sleeve. "Bugs," she said.

The old man turned with a start, appearing shocked to find her beside him. "What?"

"Bugs. You're letting them in the door."

He pulled his arm away and shooed her back into the kitchen, saying, "We're going out for a minute. Me and Clay."

Clay put up his hands in a show of weariness, but the old man insisted. "I need to show you something," he said. "Something important." Then he shook the keys and waved for Clay to follow.

"Go on," Ellie told him, even though Clay had already started for the door. He paused there while his grandfather hurried off to the pick-up parked in the driveway.

"I'll be right back," Clay said to Ellie. "You're doing great. Just keep an eye on your brother."

"Where is he?"

Clay shrugged and rolled his eyes. "Christ only knows. For somebody the size of a small moon, he can sure disappear in a hurry."

"You said something to him, didn't you?"

"Me?" He took her hand and pressed it gently. "She's harmless, you know."

"Who?"

"Gretta. There's nothing to worry about."

"Do I look worried?"

"Bugs!" Gretta yelled from somewhere in the kitchen. "The bugs are stealing all the food!"

"Just don't forget to come back," Ellie said. "Please."

Clay's grandfather fired up the truck and honked the horn.

"It's coming together, babe," Clay said to her. "A little bit of the killer instinct, and we'll be home free."

"Story of my life."

The truck was relatively new—a year removed from the assembly line at most. The vinyl dashboard still bore the glazed, wet look that reminded Clay of an unbroken saddle. Except for a discarded Slim Jim wrapper on the floorboard, the cab was spotless. Everglade air freshener, heavy and lethargic, scented the air.

"Well?" his grandfather said, motioning around the cab. "What do you think?"

"It's nice. Roomy."

"Not the truck. Me. Me driving at night."

Clay did his best to sound enthused. "Very impressive."

"Yes, well," the old man said proudly. "It clears out the cobwebs. I think I've hit every square inch of road in the county. Hell, most of Ryan County, too. There's just something about driving somewhere—*going* somewhere—but not being able to see too far ahead, you know?"

"Sure. Absolutely."

They drove back through the square, latching on to the lone road south. In a few minutes, they were free of the town and back in the desert. A sign grimly informed them of a border checkpoint several miles up ahead. On either side of the road, great slabs of rock, trimmed with sage brush, rose out of the darkness like the partially clad carcasses of giants. Clay pretended to stare straight ahead, but kept an eye trained on the key chain jangling from the ignition switch.

"So how does Gretta feel," he said, "about you leaving her alone every night?"

"Aaaah," the old man answered, sighing and waving his hand as if to disperse a whiff of smoke between them. "Gretta's been having her ups and downs these last few years. Same as always. Let's face it, her engine doesn't pass inspection."

"She's gotten worse. Is she seeing a doctor?"

The old man didn't seem to hear. "She just doesn't understand me anymore," he said with enough sadness to cause his lips to quiver. "And I mean that literally. I could be standing right in front of her, and she doesn't understand that I'm there. She just walks forward and bumps into me."

"Where are we going?"

"Day after day, it's the same. And then—" The old man snapped his fingers. "She'll get some wild notion in her head. Like it's burning a hole in there. And the funny thing is, sometimes she actually makes perfect sense. Like one of them fortune tellers. Just the other day, she—Aha!" The old man jammed on the brake with both feet. Clay threw out his hands in an effort to brace himself. The truck slid to a crooked stop in the center of the road.

"There, you see 'em?" the old man said, pointing off into the shadows. Out in the desert, a dozen dark and weary shapes moved in single file through the moonlight. Some appeared to be carrying gigantic bundles on their backs.

"Wets," the old man said. "Smugglers, too. Look at 'em. They don't even try to hide. That's how fearless they are now. I mean, we could be the Migras, right?"

"Maybe they think we're just two guys in a truck," Clay said.

His grandfather goosed the engine and started down the road again. "These smugglers, I tell you," he said. "Anything you want you can get these days. Gretta wanders out on weekends and buys all kinds of junk from them. She's turned the house into a goddamn ceramic zoo!"

"Good for the pawn business," Clay said.

The old man laughed in agreement. "Can you imagine if I still had the shop? The stuff they'd be bringing in? I had some guy offer me a python the other day. A full-grown python! And I was just standing on the street corner." He flicked on the interior light. "I mean, look at me," he said. "Is this the face of a man in need of a python?"

Clay didn't look at his grandfather. He stared straight ahead and said: "You didn't bring me out here to talk about pythons, Howard."

The old man took a long, weak breath and cleared his throat. "I've got something to tell you. Two things actually." He paused and flicked off the interior light. "It has to do with why you came back."

Clay glanced sideways. The old man's features were twisted up and crowded in the day-glo light of the dashboard, as though he had just eaten something sour. "I'm listening," Clay said.

"Gretta and I. We didn't have to take you in when your mom passed on. There wasn't any law that said we had to."

"You don't have to say this," Clay said. "Really, I understand—"

"Can I finish?" The old man was panting, struggling to speak, licking his pale lips. "If I don't get it all out in one go, it ain't going to get said."

Clay remained quiet.

"Anyway, since we didn't do such a great job with your mom, we naturally had a few reservations. Especially you being a wild one and all. The point is, we did take you in. We *did*. And except for the night you left, I don't think we caused much damage."

"Howard—"

"I mean look at yourself. You with a good job and a wife."

"Howard—"

"But that last night." Howard coughed and shook his finger out at the road ahead. "You taking a swing at Gretta. I had to go hard on you. For your own good."

"That's not why I left."

"I mean, stealing is one thing."

"Who said anything about stealing?"

"But hurting your mother is something else."

"She's not my mother."

"If I let you get away with that one, ugly act of violence . . . if I look the other way . . . then what would you be in ten years? You'd be a criminal, that's what. A murderer even. Hell, it's basic mathematics."

The old man's eyes were tearing up now. He swiped at them with the back of his hand and looked startled at the wetness he found there. "But I guess what I'm trying to say is that those were bad terms to part on. I just hope you see it like I see it. And if you can't see it like that, well . . ."

Clay didn't want to argue. But he didn't want to see the old man cry either. So he said, "It wasn't the whipping, Howard. It was the belt you used."

"The belt?"

"But look, it's all in the past, so let's just—"

"I was whipping you. What was I supposed to use?"

Clay tried, but couldn't stop the words from spilling out. "I gave you that belt as a birthday present, remember?" he said. "I probably deserved to get the shit kicked out of me for what I did, but not with a birthday present. You don't beat a kid with the present he gave you for your birthday. When you're put in charge of a kid, that's understood."

Howard was nodding back with confidence. "Yes, well, it's also understood that a kid doesn't steal a belt from his grandfather's shop and then give it to him as a present."

Clay looked over at him.

The old man smiled and shook his finger at the road again. "Didn't think I knew, did you?"

"I bought that belt."

"No, *I* bought the belt. Some pecan farmer couldn't pay his bills and hawked the thing along with a couple of tractors and a gold watch. I remember the belt because it was pure leather and had the man's initials stamped behind the buckle clasp. Lo and behold I should get it for my birthday a couple days later."

Clay gazed out at where the old man was pointing. The road ahead looked sweaty in the headlights. "I don't remember that," he said feebly.

"Who would?" The old man cleared his throat again, this time with a ragged cough, and said, "Look, like I said, stealing's one thing, so forget about it. Just forget about it."

"I have."

"Good. That's good."

"It is good."

Both men fell silent. Up ahead, the road gradually came to life. First, a few street lamps appeared, followed by more signs that announced the imminent appearance of the U.S.–Mexico

Border, across which spanned the *Colonel Truman Cross Memorial Bridge*. Clay could just make out the weary, mechanical buildings of the crossing when his grandfather eased the truck to a crawl, then whipped it around toward home, its tires biting into the gravel shoulder.

When Clay couldn't stand the quiet anymore, he said, "So what was the other thing you wanted to tell me?"

His grandfather made no move to answer. Clay was about to repeat his question when the old man said, "Gretta got arrested."

"She got *what?*"

"Yep. My wife, the felon. All because of those punks next door."

"Who? The Richardsons?"

"Oh no, they're not the Richardsons anymore. The Richardsons died two years ago. Nasty car wreck out on fifty-two. A week before Christmas, no less. And what a Christmas present that ungrateful punk kid of theirs got. Oh boy, what a Christmas present. We're talking the house, a hefty retirement account."

"Howard, what happened with Gretta?"

"She shot him."

"Shot who?"

"Him. The Richardson kid. The punk who thinks he's a rock star. Hell, what's-his-name . . ."

"Joey?"

"Joey, that's it. She pegged him with my .22 from the bedroom window. He was throwing one of his all night punk kid parties in the backyard. Pegged him right in the ass is what she did."

Clay sat dumbfounded. "My god, *why?*"

The old man shrugged. "She had plenty of legitimate reasons, God knows. Even the sheriff said so. The guy's been dealing drugs right out of his parents' home, God rest them."

"Yes, but why?"

"She said . . ." The old man paused to collect himself. "She *claimed* he was being attacked by a lion, and that she was aiming for the lion."

Without thinking, Clay felt over the bulge of bullets in his pants pocket as if to make sure they were still there. He thought about Ellie and the .22 rifle in the upstairs closet. "Jesus, this is too bizarre."

His grandfather agreed. "I told the county sheriff, 'Raid 'em.' Who knows what kind of mind weed they got growing in the basement. For all I know, that nut went out and bought a lion with the inheritance. Is that possible?"

"I don't think so," Clay said.

"Jesus, listen to me. I sound like Gretta. Anyway, I was going to put her somewhere. In a home for, you know, people like her, before something serious happens—"

Clay cut him off. "Before—? Before something—?" Clay had to take a deep breath before finishing. "Jesus, Howard, she could have killed him."

"Sure she could have."

"So what happened to your golden rule? About not hurting people?"

"I didn't say people. I said, mothers. Or grandmothers in your case. Jesus, it wasn't like I *made* her do it."

Clay leaned toward the open window, trying to get air that suddenly seemed to be eluding him. "Why?" he said, shaking his head.

"I told you, she thought she saw a—"

"No, no. Why me? Why are you telling *me*?"

The old man's lips quivered again. He licked at them before saying, "Because I'm not well. And because Gretta's Gretta. And because you're here. And because I guess I need you to . . . I need you to . . ."

Clay spoke quickly, with finality, in hopes his grandfather wouldn't finish the statement. "Whatever you need, Howard. Whatever you need, okay?"

"I need you to take us in." The old man started to say more, but instead, he began to cry again, silent and unsettling. His thin shoulders shook and his hands gripped the wheel fiercely.

It was all Clay could do to keep from screaming. A taut anger swept over him, but he managed to say, with a calm that surprised and even scared him: "Like I said, whatever you need."

The old man sniffled. "I knew it," he said. "I knew you'd help. I knew when I heard your voice on the phone. I said to Gretta—"

"We should head back," Clay said. "Really, it's time to head back."

"We are heading back."

"That's good."

The old man was drying his face with his sleeve. "It is good," he said, sniffling. "It is."

Once back at the house, Clay made a point to linger beside the truck for a moment, kicking the tires, pretending to appreciate them. He then fell in behind his grandfather, watching as the old man plopped the key ring down on a credenza in the foyer. Clay removed his jacket and draped it over the keys to muffle the sound, then reached under with one hand and slid them out. He pressed the keys deep into his pocket just as Ellie emerged from the kitchen to greet them.

From the look on her face, they couldn't have arrived a moment too soon. Clay could hear his grandmother shouting from the kitchen. "Is that him? Is he finally here? Don't let him into the dining room! It's not ready yet!"

Howard sighed, offered Ellie a shrug and walked into the kitchen. "Time to downshift, Gretta," he said. "I need you to downshift before you overheat."

Ellie embraced Clay, whispering urgently that Lem was still nowhere to be found.

"Maybe the neighborhood lions hit the jackpot," Clay said.

Ellie glared at him. "If you said anything to make him run away," she threatened.

"He's already a runaway."

"If that's what you think . . . maybe I should leave too."

"Ellie," he said, speaking tightly through his smile. "The keys are in my pocket. We're close."

"Not without my brother, we're not."

Howard reappeared at the kitchen door, his bony fingers clasped around a frayed photo album. He reached out for Ellie's hand. "Time we got acquainted, little miss," he said.

Ellie smiled back at him, but needed a small push from Clay to get her to take the old man's hand. Clay followed the two into the living room. Instead of sitting down with them, he stretched his arms and said, "Gotta run to the little boys room."

"We haven't moved it since you left," his grandfather said, cracking open the photo album so that half of it stretched across Ellie's legs.

Clay took the stairs by twos. On the way down the hall, he hooked an arm into the bathroom to crank on the water faucet and switch on the light. Pen light in mouth, he slipped once again into his grandparents' bedroom. There, in the spineless dark, he paused. Through the vent, he heard their voices, humming like radio fuzz. Howard was referencing a photo in the album. "And this is my old truck. . . . See, that's Clay there. . . . I swear I couldn't keep him away from that old truck . . ."

Beyond this, from the dining room, Gretta was calling out to nobody in particular—"Perfect! Come see, everyone!" This was followed by a slight pause in which nobody in particular acknowledged her, followed, in turn, by her waving off the imaginary stampede with, "Wait, hold it, not yet! Not quite finished!"

Clay flipped on the pen light with his tongue and plunged into the pool of light cast over his grandparents' bed. He knifed his hand under the comforter, feeling for the pillows. He stripped away two pillow cases, fitting one inside of the other and punching the bottom to test its strength.

In the closet, his work was complicated by sweat streaming into his eyes. It took him several tries to find the right key. All the while, he was certain he was taking too long. His heart took to pounding upward into his chest, as though a small spring kept uncoiling there. In a way, he wasn't as much afraid of being caught as he was of finding nothing in the footlocker when he opened it.

But Clay wasn't disappointed. He stared down at a simmering treasure of hawked and much-handled jewelry—strings of pearls, rings, heaps of gold chains—collected over the years from a thousand desperate owners, a thousand debtors. Clay dug his fingers down into the treasure, pulling gummy handfuls out and depositing them as quietly as possible into the pillow cases. It wasn't long before his forearm strained from the work and his fingers began to scrape the wood bottom of the chest.

There, beneath the spoils, he clawed up a lone picture frame that enclosed his own youthful face. It was his high school picture, and he was aping a grin for the camera, his eyes bright and not quite awake. The collar of his shirt was white and crisp. Gretta Hamilton had always washed clothes as fanatically as she cooked because you just never knew when guests were going to stop by. Clay turned the photo over and read the short message scribbled in ballpoint on the cardboard backing. It read, *Clay Patrick Hamilton—eleventh grade—straight C's, one D.* The script belonged to his grandfather.

Clay turned the picture back over and marveled at the boy he once was, teetering on the edge of what he could be and what he would be. "They're gonna write that on your tombstone, buddy," he whispered to himself, the pen light muffling the words. "Straight C's, one D, and still he fucked up." He started to put the photo back, but stopped. He glanced once more at the picture, then shoved it deep into the pillow case which was now bulging outward across the floor.

Leaving only a scattering of trinkets, Clay secured the trunk, then made his way toward the small window that faced the strip of lawn between his house and the house next door. He had to use both hands to haul the sack of booty. For one terrified moment, he thought the window might be nailed shut, if only to prevent Gretta from taking pot shots at the neighbors. But the window easily slid open. He muscled the sack over the ledge, held it aloft for a moment, and let it fall into the darkness below. Clay didn't listen for the impact. Instead, he immediately shut the window and rushed out into the hallway. He paused at the bathroom, once more hooking his arm through the door to shut off the water. The toilet, he flushed with this foot.

Ellie's eyes appealed to him for support as soon as he came down the stairs. She had inched away from his grandfather who was now more or less showing the pictures to himself. "This is me and Clay in Fort Worth," he was saying. "Look at us. Put our scalps together and you'd have one head of hair if that."

Clay winked at her and slid into the club chair.

His grandfather glanced up. "Clay, you remember Fort Worth, don't you? We went up there to—Jesus." The old man's thin face folded up with concern that mirrored Ellie's. "You're sweating a flash flood, boy."

Clay dabbed his forehead with the back of his hand. He was stunned to find the skin there sopping. "It's hot," he offered with a lame smile.

"Been hot all day. Your body just figure that out?"

"Guess I'm not feeling well either. We've been on the road a long time."

Gretta appeared at his side. She wore an oven mitt on each hand and stared down at him with a vague recognition. "You don't look right, honeybunch," was her diagnosis.

Clay nodded as though to dismiss her, but the old woman reached out with the oven mitt, running it over the top of his head, pushing his thin wet hair back. "You're not sick though," she said in a low, drugged tone more akin to a dream. "You're scared."

Clay produced an uneasy laugh and tried to fend off the oven mitt. But Gretta kept it pressed firmly on him. Her hand was strong and the mitt soft and oddly comforting. A sudden clarity washed across her face. "What reason could you have to be scared, honeybunch?" she said. "Don't you know you're safe with us?"

"I'm not scared, Gretta. Now if you don't mind—"

Gretta snatched her hand back suddenly. Her eyes bulged and she shook the oven mitt from her hand as though it were afire. Gone from her face was any semblance of sympathy or compassion. Now she was horrified. Now she was sucking at the air with short, quick breaths. She pinched the collar of her blouse tight around her throat as if to keep out a chill. "What have you done?" she gasped. "What have you done?"

"Nothing," Clay said, again with uneasy smile. But he had spoken too quickly and his grandfather, not moving, narrowed his eyes. "Gretta, now," the old man said.

Gretta took a step back. She pointed at Clay, her finger hooked and impoverished with age. "He's going to murder us, Howard."

"Take it easy, Gretta."

But the old man's half-hearted attempt to calm her only managed to convince Gretta that what she was seeing was real. She shook her head and her voice rose in alarm. "There's no way around it, is there? You've *got* to kill us both. It's the only way you'll get away with it now."

"Clay. . . ." Ellie was on her feet now.

"Get away with what?" the old man said.

Clay turned to him. "Jesus, Howard, c'mon. Don't encourage her."

"That's what the fat man is for, isn't it?" Gretta shouted. "He's outside now. Digging our graves." She whirled to face her husband. "Don't just sit there, Howard. For God's sake, they're going to murder us both!"

The old man's eyes moved from Gretta to Clay—balancing between complete belief and utter embarrassment. Finally, he looked up, over Clay's shoulder, his eyes sharpening to slits as though some profound thought or realization had just occurred to him.

"Listen," Ellie said. Her face appeared drained of blood. "Why don't we all just—"

The old man tossed the photo album aside, stood up, and clawed the drawer open beside him. He dug out the .38 revolver, even as Clay was reaching for him. "Goddamn ungrateful son of a bitch!" he muttered.

"Howard, Jesus," Clay said, but his words were swallowed by Gretta's shrieks. "Yes! Shoot them, Howard! Shoot them all before it's too late!"

Clay could only raise his hands, mouth agape, and watch as the old man fumbled to get a firm grip on the gun. He thumbed back the hammer and leveled the gun vaguely at Clay. "Ungrateful little bastard! I told you to stay clear of my property!"

Clay finally realized that the old man wasn't even addressing him. His shouts were meant for someone else, someone on the other side of the window, someone in the backyard. "Goddamn little shit, I'll put a third hole in your ass!"

Ellie, just slightly more aware than Clay, shouted, "Jesus, it's Lem. Please, no, he's not—that's my brother! It's my brother!"

Clay and Gretta turned together just as the sliding glass door rattled open. Lem teetered on the threshold for a moment, then shouldered his way in through the opening. His face was puffed and glassy with sweat and a splinter of blood ran across his forehead. His lumbering progress through the door was hindered by the fact that he was dragging something from behind.

Ellie swept forward, her arms raised up, repeating three times that the injured intruder was her brother. Her voice squeaked with alarm.

"Her brother," Clay confirmed for his grandfather.

The old man lowered the gun and moved forward to help, saying, "Her—what's he doing out back?"

Clay simply shrugged and began probing his temples with the points of his fingers in an effort to calm himself. It was at that moment, with his grandfather jostling a chair out from the table, that Clay recognized the burden that Lem was dragging. It was the pillow sack, streaked with dirt and heavy with treasure.

Desperately, Clay scrambled forward, a second too late. His grandfather had already taken the sack from Lem's hand. He took it without any realization of what it was, but rather as a host might relieve a weary traveler of a suitcase.

"Have a seat," the old man said. Ellie helped her brother down into the chair.

Gretta lingered behind them all, her voice transformed from the ringing terror it had been just a moment before to a lofty calm. "Yes, sit," she said. "You're just in time. My grandson is coming for a visit. He's bringing his new wife."

With a stunned, confused expression, Lem recounted what had happened to him. "I snuck one of the pig-in-a-blankets," he said, gesturing at the table. "Or maybe it was a couple. I tried to eat it real fast and started to choke. I didn't want to get in trouble so I went outside . . . around the side of the house. The last thing I remember was that I was pounding on my chest, trying to get it out. I couldn't breathe. . . . "

Ellie was dabbing his forehead with the napkin. Beneath the blood, the swollen shadow of a bruise stood out.

"I guess I fainted," Lem said. He felt over his throat. "It must have popped loose when I hit the ground."

"You're damn lucky," Howard told him. "I hardly ever go back there. You could have been out there for days. Hell, for years."

Lem agreed. "So the next thing I know," he said, "I'm in this weird dream. I'm laying on the ground and I'm sleeping and I feel this big wet tongue on my face and I open my eyes and there's this lion licking me. He's just licking my face, right, and I'm laying there trying to get back to sleep, but I can't because this freaking lion keeps licking my face, you know?" Lem scoffed as if to say it was a common problem that anyone could appreciate. "And that's when I finally woke up."

Clay positioned himself just behind his grandfather. He attempted to ease the pillow case from the old man's grip. "Here, let me take this," he said.

But the old man held on, even tugging roughly away. "What is this?"

Lem just looked at the sack and shrugged wearily. "It was on top of my chest," he said. "It's heavy."

The old man peeled open the sack and peered inside. He stared down in silence for a moment, then shook it up and down as if testing its weight. Finally, he reached inside, using the barrel of the .38 to stir up the contents. "Good god," he whispered to himself.

"Howard," Clay said.

But the old man had already turned his eyes away from the sack as though its contents were blinding. He twisted the opening closed and, never taking his eyes off the floor, extended it out toward Clay. "This is yours," he said.

"Howard—"

"No, take it. Go on. It's what you came here for."

"Do you have any ice?" Ellie said to Gretta.

"Ice?" Gretta said. She touched her husband's sleeve from behind, as if seeking his support. "No, I'm afraid we only have enough ice for our guests."

"That's okay," Clay said."We don't need ice."

"That's good," the old man said roughly, his mouth settling into a grimace. He seemed to be struggling to keep from coughing. "That's good because we don't have any for you."

Gretta nodded confidently. "That's always the story, isn't it?" she said to all of them and to none of them. "There's just no way to keep enough of what you need most. Too many guests. Too many guests . . ."

It wasn't until they were back in the Olds that Clay realized he still had his grandfather's keys in his pocket. He looked back at the house to see if anyone was peeking out the windows. He had no idea what he should do with the keys. Taking them back— even tossing them into the mailbox—seemed an impossibility.

"We can't just leave," Ellie was saying to him. "Can we?"

"We got what we came for," Clay said.

"Yes, but we can't just let them call the police."

"My head," Lem groaned from the back seat. "Jesus, it's starting to hurt."

Clay turned and regarded Ellie. He tried to find her eyes in the darkness, but they were lost in shadow. "What are you saying?" he said to her.

She patted the sack of jewels on the seat between them. "I'm saying what's the point of having this . . . if we just get arrested down the road."

"Is anyone hearing me?" Lem said. "I might need medical attention here, folks."

Clay shut his eyes and sighed as if in pain.

"I could say I forgot something," Ellie continued. "Lem could stay here. We could go back inside together. I'm not saying you have to do it alone. I would be right there with you, babe."

"Enough," Clay said. "Okay? Enough." He cranked the engine and let the motor idle.

"Look, I don't want to go to jail," Ellie said. "And I don't want my brother to go to jail. They could be calling the police right now. I mean, I thought that's what the gun was for in the first place."

"What gun?"

"*Your* gun. Your gun under the seat."

"Why in the fuck-shit-hell," Clay yelled at her, "would I leave it under the seat if I was going to use it!"

"Baby, baby," Ellie said in a soothing tone. She reached out and began pressing at the back of Clay's neck. "You don't even have to do it, babe. If you want—If you need me to . . ."

"Enough!" Clay rammed his foot down on the accelerator. Their heads were thrown back as the Olds lurched forward toward the dead-end sign, beyond which an endless dark desert unfolded like a ravenous black hole. Clay cut the wheel hard, and the Olds fish-tailed into a neat U-turn, straightening out amid a swirl of smoked rubber. They were just moving forward, on the verge of picking up speed, when Clay cried out once and slammed on the brakes.

A full-grown lion stood in the middle of the road, directly in their path. The giant cat appeared scrawny and tired in the spray of headlights. Frothy spit dripped from its mouth and a single length of chain hung limply from its neck, snaking down across the road at its feet. The beast lowered its head, huffed once at them, then pushed off into the desert night, dragging the chain behind, churning up a path of dust.

Lem was the first to shatter the numb silence. "That's the one. Sweet Jesus, that's the one that licked me." He sat back and slapped his forehead. "Holy shit. He was just trying to save me."

"Or eat you," Clay said, dumbly.

Just then, a thin teenager scrambled through the headlights. He was naked save for a pair of cut-off jeans, faded and frayed at the edges. He carried what appeared to be a rope or whip and never so much as glanced at the Olds or its stunned occupants. He was in and out of the headlights, moving at a fast clip despite the fact that he was clearly hindered by a limp. He headed off in the general direction the lion had gone.

Clay watched him run after the beast. He expected the youth to vanish as quickly as the lion, but it took over a minute for the darkness to swallow the chalk white color of his skin. Clay couldn't imagine either of them—man or beast—ever coming out of that darkness again. He couldn't imagine either of them ever wanting to.

THE FIFTH WEEK

It is the fifth week of military training.

there is an inside and an outside

The fifth week out of six. We know the routine—if it can be called that

it can't

—so well that we can now envision seeing our homes again, embracing our loved ones,

or a temporary loved one

passing the day without a shave, sleeping in ruthlessly. Little do we know, most recruits get recycled in their fifth week. It would surprise us to know this. We believe, in the fifth week, that we are beyond surprise.

Our T. I.

technical instructor

is Sergeant Richards. We know him as "Sir," officially, but it is understood that he is God.

the angry, puritanical version

He has finished yelling at us for the day, and we are left in charge of the dormitory. This is relieving.

there is no relief here

In the first four weeks, he yelled at us all day and all night and no one could get any sleep. Sometimes, when he got tired of yelling, he would order us to yell at ourselves.

we are the filthiest form of scum, we should be shot as a favor to our country

But this happens rarely. Sgt. Richards, like God, seldom tires of yelling.

There are other freedoms available to us on this day in the fifth week. We are permitted to use the telephone.

once

We only have so much time, and there is only one phone. There are many of us; so we all agree to talk for one minute and if a recruit takes longer than one minute, he will be beaten and humiliated in the shower that evening, and will be given an embarrassing nickname. Nicknames are very important here, so no one wants this to happen to them. One recruit had to have his bunk sprayed in the first week, and despite all his efforts to prove himself worthy of pity, he became known—and will always be known—as "Crab Crotch." He was recycled in the third week. The nickname followed him to his next unit. One day, his mother will call him by that name.

We stand in line for the phone which sits in the corner of the day room. We talk to our parents, our wives, our children, our dogs. Some recruits have none of these things

or believe these things beyond control

and make a small fortune selling off their minutes. A dollar for a quarter minute, take it or leave it.

Possum gets off the phone and looks extremely concerned. He had called his parents, but had talked to his brother instead. His brother did not have good news for him.

Big Foot asks him what's wrong.

My poodles, Possum says.

Poodles? Tex says. What the hell do you want with poodles?

Possum says, I gave my parents written instructions on how to deal with Roger and Tuffy. What day they like their baths. How much Alpo to feed them so they don't get stomach aches. They promised to take care of them for me. I made them swear.

Applehead walks up to the group, head crooked to the side as if he is still on the phone. He is beaming so brightly that he immediately attracts all the attention. My wife just went into labor, he says. I called just in time to hear her scream at me.

What did she scream? Hamburger asks.

You should've heard her, Applehead says. It's got sores, she said. I told her, it doesn't have sores, honey. And she said, You dumb bastard, it's got sores! Applehead laughs

no one smiles here

at the memory. It is obvious that he will squeeze—as we all will—every last drop of blood from the one-minute call.

My wife did the same thing when she had our kid, says Hamburger. Called me every name in the book. What a night!

Good thing I'm here and not there, Applehead says. He becomes suddenly confused, though not from his last comment

for which he rightfully deserves confusion

He feels over his lumpy, shaved head. What the hell was that supposed to mean anyway? he asks himself aloud. Why would it have sores?

You must have heard her wrong, Big Foot says.

She probably said, it's got *pores*, Hamburger says. Women notice stupid details like that when they're having kids.

Applehead nods fearfully. The connection *was* bad, he says.

We all turn back to Possum who is still in shock and seems not to have heard anything outside of his skull. Tex tells him to go on. With his story.

So my parents swore, Possum goes on. Even as they drove me to the airport, they were swearing. The dogs came with us and I cried pretty hard when I said goodbye to Tuffy, but more with

Roger because he wouldn't even look at me. He gets like that. But here's the thing: After they dropped me off, they drove straight to the vet and had my poodles put to sleep. They didn't even stop once. They went straight there.

Everyone takes a step backward, to give Possum some room.

a little room is a great gift here

Only Tex moves forward. He puts his arm around Possum. Listen, he says sagely, you can't let this get to you. Poodles are for pussies anyway. Your parents did you a favor, believe me.

Barney Rubble joins our group. He had no one to call, and he is counting a handful of money with one hand. The reason he is only using one hand is because his other hand is on his head. Earlier that day, Sgt. Richards saw him walk out of a building without his fatigue cap, so Barney was ordered to walk around all day with one hand on his head. Technically, it isn't necessary that he continue to do so since Sgt. Richards isn't around, but a recruit in his fifth week—like a monk on his deathbed—takes no chances. Barney sees Possum and demands to know who pissed on his parade. He is a dangerous man, that Barney Rubble.

They're evil, Possum says, tears pumping from his eyes

not unusual here

I'll kill them when I get back. That's what I'll do. I'll use my training and put *them* to sleep.

Why don't you just show them your dick, Barney says. Isn't that how you put your girlfriend to sleep?

Tex asks Barney if it's possible to be so funny with a boot sticking up his ass.

I'm here for my country, right? Possum says. And this is how they thank me? His voice has gone hoarse; his eyes vibrate strangely, like a mechanical human's eyes would vibrate if it suddenly began to malfunction.

Calm down, we warn him. Breathe.

Oh sweet Mary of Christ, Applehead says. His mouth is wide open. He is white and sweatless. She didn't say, it's got sores. She said, it's not yours. It's not yours!

Possum breaks for the phone. He kicks aside the recruit who happens to be talking on it.

I'm going to give them something to think about, Possum yells, recklessly stabbing numbers into the phone. I'm going to tell them they're as good as dead! When I get through with them, they'll—

He doesn't finish the sentence because we are upon him. A muffled, deliberate mob of barracks justice.

a rumor

No one hits him in the face, but everyone hits him. Many, many times. Barney, one hand clutching a wad of cash, the other planted on his head, does not hit Possum. He kicks him instead.

That night, with everyone snoring

or weeping

in their bunks, Applehead unlaces one of his boots, sneaks past the dorm guard and into the latrine. He stands on one of the heads, secures the bootlace to an overhead pipe, ties the other end around his neck, and jumps. The bootlace immediately breaks, and he falls to the ground, spraining his ankle. The dorm guard wakes up the CQ over the incident, and two security policemen come and take Applehead away in his underwear,

limping

the bootlace still imbedded in the soft flesh of his neck. Applehead was to be a munitions systems specialist.

a bomb builder

If his wife had not borne another man's child, Applehead might have killed us all.

We sleep; we dream of this woman, this savior. We decorate her with our crimes.

The next morning, Possum does not make his bunk properly. He remains upset about the poodles and has coughed up blood all night although this is no one's fault but his own.

fault is never deferred here

Sgt. Richards yells at everyone, and we must strip and remake our beds several times until we get it right

there is no "right"

We formulate a plan

telepathically

to let Possum host a blanket party that will surely cripple him. We love Possum

more than his parents do

but only to the point where our survival is threatened. Weakness in the lifeboat adrift

there is no other comparison

is dinner served. Luckily for everyone, Possum is told to pack up his shit and is recycled to another unit two weeks behind us. His is a fate so dreaded that he is never spoken of again.

That afternoon, when we return from chow, we find that Applehead's bunk has been stripped. His locker stands open and empty. They have taken him to a place called Mental Health. It is worse than being recycled, they say. No one ever returns from Mental Health. We do not feel sorry for him,

we cannot afford to part with sorrow

but we find some consolation in the fact that we are not him and he is not us.

Sgt. Richards calls us together in the day room. We spring to attention when he walks in, although we were well prepared to do so; the steel taps on his heels prophesy his coming. He glides on his taps. His light blue uniform is crisp and meaningful. On every part of his body, there are corners and slants, as if he were an image created by a computer. Even his face has no roundness, only edges. He is fatless, pure.

He tells us to sit the fuck down. We do, cross-legged on the cold floor like a tribe of camouflaged, Buddhist monks. There are chairs in the room but we are not good enough for them. Only recruits in their sixth week are good enough for the chairs. Some of us, it is becoming profoundly clear, will never be good enough for them.

Sgt. Richards explains that he is very unhappy with Airman Johnson's

Applehead's

attempted suicide. I'm a laughing stock with the other T. I.s, he says. If you're going to do it, at least have the courtesy to do it right. He holds up an imaginary razor blade, and he instructs, with the same intensity he has instructed us to prepare for our future, how to efficiently, militarily commit suicide. Down, he says, not across. You have to slash down to get the vein. Otherwise, you'll make a fool out of me. And I don't like being a fool.

Then he does something he has never done before. He asks us if we have any questions about what he has just told us.

No one asks a question.

those who would have asked a question at that moment were eliminated in the first week

I hate you, he says to our perfect silence. I hate all of you. You are worse than women; you are little girls.

We look back at him with the strongest, wettest love that can be drawn from sane minds.

only the inside matters

We would die for him if we thought it would please him.

LAST KNOWN POSITION
2,000 Feet Above the World and Descending

It was while jogging the scarred mountain road above the town of San Luis, Argentina, that I came upon a boy and his horse. Judging by the skid marks and stench of burnt rubber, the two had had a very close encounter with a very large truck. Such encounters were common in the desolate region—about the only thing Argentines did fast was drive—and rarely ended happily. I saw no promise that this case would be the exception.

The boy stood at the extreme bend in the road, peering out over a sheer drop of some 500 feet. His foot rested on a guardrail that appeared to be made of greasy tin foil. I put his age at no more than a decade, despite the fact that the setting sun cast a streak of severe maturity across his features. He wore a crumpled cowboy hat pulled snug across the line of his brow. His jeans were torn open at one knee and a small crosshatch of blood glistened within. As far as I could tell, this was his only injury.

The horse's wounds were not so easy to identify since it occupied a space of air several feet beyond the guardrail. It had apparently chosen to leap off the cliff rather than face the on-rushing truck. But instead of plunging to its death, the beast had landed atop a lone alamo tree that grew crookedly from the cliff face and extended out over the bluff. The massive body of the horse was now entangled within a net of thick, leafless branches. Its legs protruded downward, straight and stiff, as if it were straining to reach the ground far below. Perhaps most incongruent—even more than a dying tree supporting such enormous weight—was the expression of utter boredom on the face of the animal. It might well have been standing in a field noshing hay than suspended high above jagged knots of rock, pampas grass, and hastily dumped garbage.

I walked the last several yards to the scene, blinking sweat from my eyes, all in hopes that what I was seeing would become as unreal as it was unbelievable. The boy recognized my astonishment and offered a sympathetic smile. When I asked him in Spanish if everything was all right, the smile dropped away from his face. He regarded me suspiciously, then jabbed a thumb at the horse and shrugged, as if to say, *Sure, except for my horse being stuck in this tree, things couldn't be better.*

"What happened to the truck?" I said.

The boy glanced off to where the road disappeared around the bend, then turned back and studied me. His eyes were wide and serious, blackened by the shade of his hat brim. Even though it was still quite warm out, his bottom lip quivered as if from a cold wind. I thought for a moment that he might be in shock. Then I realized he was simply reading the logo on the front of my sweat-soaked T-shirt. *Nike*, he mouthed several times. Finally, in decent English, he asked if I were one of the American F-16 pilots visiting the Air Base in San Luis. When I nodded, he told me that he had read about me in his English class, in an English-language newspaper. His name was Miguel, he said, and the horse's name was, of all things, *Aguila*. Eagle. Without paying the slightest homage to this irony, he again gestured to the horse moored to the side of the cliff, and said, "This does not happen in America, *verdad?*"

I stared back at the boy. Taking care to speak slowly, clearly, I said to him: "This doesn't happen anywhere, my friend."

Miguel adjusted his hat and nodded. "It has," he said with a weary sigh, "now happened here."

Our squadron commander called us "goodwill ambassadors." Any airman worth his stripes could see that the mission was nothing more than an intercontinental sales pitch. We were to fly a dozen F-16s down to San Luis Air Base and line them up beside Argentina's aging A-4s, the ones that leaked fuel faster than they could suck it in. It was our way of showing our new allies what they were missing and what they could have—watered-down versions anyway—for the nominal price of 30 million pesos a pop. This was not to say the Argentine Air Force wasn't well aware of what they were missing. Thanks to the Islas Malvinas War, as the Argentines called the Falklands War, their pilots were still considered the best the continent had to offer. In fact, they could barely contain their embarrassment at having to fly formations next to our jets, knowing our pilots were cruising at half-throttle.

Luckily, my job didn't entail salesmanship. Contrary to my suggestion to Miguel, I did not fly F-16s. My bird was a monstrosity called a C-141 Starlifter. A glorified cargo plane used to haul supporting ground crews and a spare engine or two. The plane's avionics were so advanced that to say it flew itself was to only mildly exaggerate. I spent more of my cockpit time mulling over my recent divorce than I did handling any controls.

This was not to say that I wasn't proud of being a pilot and the status it afforded. But let's face it: guys who drive pick-ups don't enjoy the status of those who drive Porsches. The two groups don't make the same kind of money or live in the same kind of house. They certainly don't marry the same kind of woman and—after finding their wife in bed with a neighbor—they don't consider it a failure when divorce goes from something you threaten to something you sign. To the top guns of the world, the "upper crust" as we called them at the academy, trust was just a fashion statement anyway, an image, a bonus if it showed up on radar. I trusted because that's what I thought trustworthy people did. And now? After I'd been fooled, cut off at the knees, hooked, reeled in and clubbed on the boat deck? What was my idea of trust now? That's easy. I wouldn't be caught dead with it.

Which was precisely why I was jogging alone in the first place. We had been told—in addition to doing our best Bob Hope while off-duty—to travel in pairs, to use the "wingman system," the surest defense against being mugged, conned or worse. But hanging around with the top guns would only serve to remind me of what I wasn't. Besides, I wasn't worried. I spoke fairly good Spanish, having grown up in West Texas, on the Mexican border. I only wanted to see the sights. To forget my mistakes. To breathe in the culture and the people.

So here I was, breathing it in like jet intake, on the edge of a mountain road faced with an obstacle only slightly more appealing than the sight of my wife in bed with another man. And as I stared at the horse wedged in the tree, I knew only one thing for certain: A great many laws of gravity and luck were being broken before my eyes and I didn't know how to apply my own knowledge and experience to change a thing.

Miguel was speaking rapidly to me now, in Spanish, a language perfectly suited to rapid speech. He had apparently formulated a plan to rescue his horse and couldn't get it out of his mouth fast enough. Although I didn't catch everything he said, I do know that the plan involved both of us working together. The plan also involved our clothes. He motioned to my shirt several times and seemed to be indicating that between us, we could construct a makeshift rope with what we were wearing.

When my mind finally caught up with his words—when I realized he was describing a jailbreak, not a rescue—I held my hand up. "First of all, you're going to need a car," I said, mindful not to volunteer the pronoun *we*. "Or maybe a truck." I wasn't sure how even a truck would help the situation, but it sounded much more appealing than stripping on a deserted road in Argentina.

"My father has truck," Miguel said, then averted his eyes as if he regretted the admission. "But he never use this truck."

"He might want to start."

Miguel was now shaking his head, completely retracting his statement. "My father," the boy said. "He is not home until later. If he knows of this, he will be very angry. Very angry." He grimaced at the thought, then looked at his bare wrist, presumably where he would have worn a watch if he had one. For some reason, the action made me instinctively glance down at the small jogging pouch Velcroed around my ankle. The pouch bulged with my wristwatch, wallet and passport.

Miguel's gaze followed mine, and as his eyes lingered at my feet, I felt suddenly unnerved. Dressed as he was, Miguel would have fit in perfectly with the street urchins that prowled the plaza of San Luis. They were crafty rogues who worked in teams of five or six. A favorite con was to use a water pistol to surreptitiously squirt green mustard on the shoulders of naive, unsuspecting *turistas*. Then they clamored around their victim, telling him that he had been crapped on by birds, offering to wipe the stain clean, all the while relieving him of his wallet and other valuables. I thought of this, then looked over at the horse and was immediately prodded by a pang of guilt. The boy had enough troubles without me silently indicting his intentions.

"I'm sure your father will understand," I said to him.

"Sí, he will understand, señor," the boy said sourly. "And then he will throw me from the cliff."

"This wasn't your fault. Hell, you're lucky to be alive."

"Sí, and I also am lucky for you to come running here, no?"

I said nothing, fueled by the sudden desire to go running the other way. But an equally insistent paralysis kept me from doing so. It rooted me to the spot with two simple words: *Goodwill Ambassador.*

As if encouraged by my silence, Miguel grew animated with yet another idea. "My sister, she will help us, but she also cannot drive my father's truck."

I shook my head, more a reflex than anything else, but Miguel insisted, pleaded. "It's okay. Pretend you are still running. My house is only one kilometer on this road. Please, señor."

I took a deep breath and relented. And very soon regretted it. The house was not one kilometer away. It was closer to three, uphill, each one more uphill than the last. As we fought the incline and winding road, the boy eagerly picked away at me. He wanted to be a pilot, he said. He wanted to fly the mighty F-16 like me, the fastest jet in the sky. He told me he would sink British ships, especially the ones loaded with British Marines. Did I know that Argentina sank two British destroyers during the Malvinas War? It would have been better, he said, if they sank the ships carrying British Marines. "That way, we would still have the islands." He paused and thought about it. "Although, it is very cold there on the islands. And there are not too many good reasons to live there."

I told him I had once heard the war described as two bald men fighting over a comb, and Miguel, to my surprise, laughed heartily.

The way he spoke, with numbed awe and excitement, reminded me of my wife when we first met. How she had marveled at my chrome pilot's wings and flight suit. To her, flying was an exotic business, salted with danger and adventure. I never lied to her about it, but as with Miguel, I did nothing to dissuade her from thinking more of me than she should have. "I'd always thought I was marrying the equivalent of a doctor," she told me later, as a way of justifying her infidelity. "But one day I woke up and realized that you're nothing like a doctor. You're just a normal person. Like a bus driver."

It was, indeed, a dark secret. Pilots weren't geniuses, and most weren't even necessarily bright people. In today's Air Force, you could train a monkey to fly a plane. At least, the kind of plane I flew.

About a half-hour into our hike, we rounded a bend that partly obscured a gravel road cutting into the hillside. The chain-link gate that guarded the road stood open, but only because it had come off its hinges. The entrance looked about as inviting as an uncovered manhole. I tried reading a sign attached to the fence, but a cloudy blue darkness had settled around us and the sign's print was faded anyway.

Miguel led me confidently up the driveway. Strewn along its flanks were heaps of wrecked autos and other dark mechanical hulks that defied definition and even looked vaguely obscene in the shadows. Piles of hubcaps and rusted bumpers also took shape in the crude trenches that bordered the road. Small animals— most likely wild guinea pigs—scurried amid the grim soup of metal and weeds.

More to make conversation than anything, I asked Miguel about the car wrecks, and he said with a smile: "No trees."

"No what?" I said.

He giggled, but stopped when he saw that I wasn't laughing with him. "Sí, no trees for to land on. That is how you say, no?"

"Ah," I said, getting it. I didn't laugh.

The road finally leveled onto a plateau, hemmed in by craggy slopes that disappeared skyward. The shadow of a perfectly square house emerged to our front. Beside this, like part of a matching set, stood a perfectly square garage. From the screen door of the main dwelling, a ghastly, plum-colored light spilled out onto the porch and down a rickety set of steps. The front windows were dark and appeared to be made of wine bottle glass. I would have guessed the whole scene uninhabited save for a lone satellite dish perched atop the roof.

We halted in front of the stairs and stood, like conspirators, completely immersed in shadows. Miguel looked around. "My father no is here," he said with a marked degree of relief. Then: "I am going to get my sister." He said this, but he did not move.

Then he looked up at me and swallowed. Although his features were barely discernible, I did see that the maturity had washed away from his face, and he now looked exactly like a boy who had done a bad thing. But there was also something else. Something that I could not get my mind around. It was even a bit sinister, in a vague, illogical way. Like the feeling of being watched, but without the faintest idea why anyone would want to. Miguel said, "You might like my sister, señor. You might like her very much."

"I might," I said, uneasy now and even irritated. "I might like your father, too. I might even like your horse. But I'm not going to be around long enough for any of that."

The boy continued to peer at me, undeterred. "She speaks English very well, my sister. She is a teacher. And many men like her." He named a few of them as if her local mileage offered proof of her value to a worldly man like me. "One of them was Jesus Fioni. He is football player who play one year for the Boca Juniors. Football, you know? That is soccer."

"I know what it is. Look, maybe you should just go get her. There's nothing to worry about. Just tell her what happened. It wasn't your fault."

Miguel licked his lips again, then motioned for me to wait. He walked gingerly up the stairs like a hen-pecked husband sneaking home after a night out with poker buddies. He wasn't half-way up when a tall woman in a loose summer dress pushed out through the screen door. I was so startled by her sudden appearance that I jumped backward.

The woman towered over the boy, commanding the top of the stairs, barring him from moving farther. She inspected him briefly, looked at me, then back at him again. From where I stood, there didn't seem to be any justification for Miguel's claim of her popularity. She appeared slim and fit, but her overall shape had the weariness that comes from a lifetime of undeserved hardships, as though her fitness had been got by carrying blocks of concrete over broken terrain. Her appearance was further complicated by a head of frizzled, witchlike black hair and wide, scowling eyes. In the shadows at least, she looked to be about thirty-five, much older than I had imagined Miguel's sister, but what did I know?

With the sweep of one hand, she demanded a full explanation from the boy. Her mouth gaped as he began to sketch out recent events. Before he could quite finish up, she cursed and slapped him. It was a roundhouse, big sister swat that rippled down his entire body. Miguel cursed weakly at her and got a backhand for his trouble. She spit out another question. He answered "sí" and was slapped. She gestured at me and demanded a quick response. He offered one and was slapped. The only criterion for her relentless punishment seemed to be that he opened his mouth and spoke.

Then, as if in grand summation, the woman loosed a fierce barrage of curses. I'd always considered good cursing as rare as good penmanship, and I must say that this woman definitely had a gift. Although the impact is somewhat lost in translation, she essentially concluded that Miguel was the equivalent of an elderly prostitute's birth canal. To this charge, he bowed his head in submission and shame.

Then the woman lowered her voice and mumbled a question to him. The only word I caught was "abuela," or grandmother. Miguel immediately shook his head in what looked like a gesture of appeasement. Then the woman stalked back inside.

As soon as she disappeared, Miguel turned and hurried down the steps. To my surprise, he was grinning. He said, "I have good news, señor. She will help us."

"Not us, Miguel," I corrected. "You. She will help *you*."

"Sí, señor. All of us."

Astounded by his upbeat demeanor, I followed him around the house to the garage, a ramshackle structure that resembled a small barn. Holes big enough to accommodate washing machines gapped across its corrugated tin roof. Its wide double doors were covered with hubcaps, nailed like animal pelts to the wooden planks.

"What did your sister mean when she asked about a grandmother?" I said to him as he struggled to pull open the door. It was caught in the gravelly threshold as though it had not been opened in years.

"Grandmother?" Miguel said and paused thoughtfully. "My grandmother no is here."

"That's not what I asked you."

"Maybe you no hear my sister right, señor."

I jammed my foot into the bottom of the door just as it was about to give way. "But maybe I did," I said.

Miguel moaned nervously. "Yes, of course, señor. I am sorry. The horse once belong to my grandmother. That is all that was meant."

We looked at each other in the dark. I waited for him to blink, for our hurried alliance to show itself for something other than what it seemed. But his innocent stare held. The woman swept up behind us, intense and business-like, a black shawl tossed around her shoulders. She snapped a scolding *"Que?"* at Miguel. He shrugged and pointed at me.

I pulled my foot from the door. In the garage, lit by a single bulb overhead, I beheld the rescue vehicle. It wasn't a truck as

I understood the word. It was more like a distant ancestor, something out of *The Waltons*. I doubted it would even start.

Miguel rummaged across a rack of shelves, threw a rope and a flashlight into the truck bed and we all piled in. The cab smelled of dust and something sour, like old orange peels. After a dozen cranks of the key, the engine finally came to life with a horrid cough—like shaking a rusty coffee can full of marbles. The non-powered steering tested several small muscles in my arms that I didn't even know I had; it took all my strength just to wield the truck down the gravel path and onto the mountain road.

"Not so fast as F-16, *verdad*?" Miguel said. He casually informed his sister—whom he called Catalina—that I flew F-16s for a living, the fastest jet in the sky. She responded with a huff, rolling down her window and tossing her frizzled hair in the breeze.

I said to her in Spanish, "Your brother is lucky to be alive."

"And the horse?" she said back in English, with an accent as thick as her attitude. "Is the horse lucky?"

"The horse is in a tree," I answered. "Where I come from that isn't luck." I thought for a moment and added, "We call that Irish Luck."

"Irish?" she said, pronouncing it, "Eereesh."

"Right, that's where you step in a pile of crap, but luckily, you're wearing an old pair of shoes." I chuckled, but the two Argentines simply stared morosely ahead.

"That was a joke," I said, with a little more resentment than was warranted.

"Maybe we are too simple for jet pilot jokes," Catalina said.

"Look," I started, fully intending to come clean, to say something like: *I'm not an F-16 pilot, okay? I fly cargo planes. I'm like a bus driver.* But I couldn't get my mouth to form any words. Miguel had taken his hat off and I could see his sister's face clearly now. It glowed in the buttery light of the dashboard and I realized that

I was looking at an absolute beauty, at a woman who possessed that rare combination of being not easily impressed and worth impressing. Her hair was curly, but not unkempt as I had thought before. And it perfectly framed the smooth skin and Castilian features of her face. Her eyes were crystallized blue in the dash lights and, turned away from me, appeared mournfully angelic, like those old paintings of dying heroes turning their eyes sky-ward, as if offering forgiveness to heaven. *Catalina*, I thought.

"Señor," Miguel said to me calmly. "It would be better for you to look at the road."

I turned back just in time to be blinded by the twin lights of a dump truck raking across the road. Its horn blared as I threw my body into the wheel, seesawing across the far lane and up onto the shoulder, scrapping the guardrail that barely managed to keep us from careening into oblivion. The two sets of bumpers missed by inches. Like a distant siren, the truck's horn faded behind us.

I swerved back onto the road, my hands gripping the wheel so hard that my knuckles audibly crackled. The only word I could emit was a breathless "Jesus."

Catalina was smiling. To Miguel, she said, "Maybe he is hoping there are enough trees for all of us."

"I say this joke to him already," Miguel said. He appeared as oblivious as she to the fact that, given one less foot of road width, we would all be dead.

She asked him, "Did he laugh?"

"He flies the fastest jet in the sky," the boy said haughtily. "He does not laugh at such nonsense."

Contrary to my darkest hopes, the horse had made no attempt to free itself and hence, had not fallen to its death and saved us the trouble of strangling it with a rope—or whatever the plan ultimately would be. There was no sign at all it had even moved. In fact, as I parked diagonally across the road, the dim splash of headlights revealed only that Aguila had fallen comfortably asleep. The animal telegraphed resignation to its fate on the highest frequency. A year from now there would be a skeleton of that horse in the tree.

I hand-cranked the brake and cut the engine. Before I could offer a chivalrous signal that it was safe to exit the truck, Catalina leapt out and scrambled over to the guardrail. Her sudden energy made me weary beyond bearing. Miguel slid out behind me, doggedly staying on my tail.

Catalina stood at the cliff edge, her hands clasped prayer-like under her chin, her shawl flapping in the breeze. She muttered something incomprehensible and nodded to herself. She had regained the same stooped stance I had seen on the porch, but now seemed oddly relaxed, even satisfied, as if what she was seeing had sated some previously insatiable need to be victimized.

"Señor?"

I spun around—almost in a complete circle—and finally located Miguel cowering behind me, determined to shield himself from the ludicrous scene he surely felt responsible for. "Señor, you will protect me, no?"

"It's going to be all right," I said, reciting what was fast becoming the official motto of the day.

His eyes moistened with tears and his bottom lip began to quiver, this time for real. "I must confess to you, señor."

I put my hand on his shoulder and told him not to worry.

"But, señor, you no understand me. I must tell you—"

"Miguel!" The woman cried out. Desperate anger now. Incapable of forgiveness.

The boy recoiled at her voice. I told him to stay were he was.

I walked up beside her, out in front of the truck. The headlights cast our shadows like black streaks of doom across the motionless horse. Beyond this, in the valley below, the lights of San Luis sparkled crudely in a pattern that was the very opposite of vibrancy. It looked like a gigantic campfire that had been stamped out or pissed out.

I set my voice to stern and fired away. "Look, I understand you're upset. But now isn't the time to blame. Now's the time to *do* something."

She was backing away from the edge now, stopping only when she butted up against the truck. She hissed a stream of Spanish at me, a language that was also perfectly suited for hissing. The brunt of what she said amounted to: "This is a terrible thing. How could he do such a terrible, terrible thing?"

"It's only terrible if we do nothing. But we're doing something. We're going to—"

Her eyes searched out mine. And when they locked on I could see in them true horror. "Miguel was on his way to pick up his grandmother," she said frantically.

Since this was new information and since I couldn't quite understand what in hell it had to do with anything, I ended up simply repeating what she had said. "He was going to pick up his grandmother? With the horse? You mean, with the horse?"

She pinched her eyes shut and said with disgust, "You can think of a better way? On his back perhaps? Or maybe it is too simple for you and your jet plane to understand—"

I cut her off, annoyed. "Fine, fine, okay? So he was going to pick up his grandmother. So what?"

She reverted back to clear, but agonizingly slow English. "He told me," she said, "that he was on his way *down* the mountain to pick her up when this happened. He was on his way down the mountain."

My ex-wife often accused me of being dense, of half-listening to her, a charge I had always hastily denied. "Auto-pilot," she had called my inattention in a fit of wit. "You put your brain on auto-pilot whenever you're faced with the ugly truth." And as it turned out, she had half a point. When I walked into that bedroom, my day-long mission scrubbed because of bad weather, and I saw her writhing in bed with her bare legs wrapped around my neighbor's hairy ass like some kind of new wrestling move, I could think of nothing better to do than pretend it wasn't happening, to pretend the mission was on, and I had let the plane take off and that I had cruised to a comfortable 35,000 feet above the world, with all its cruelty and betrayal, up in the clouds, where the computer is in charge yet no one knows it but me and the co-pilot.

And even though I was only about 2,000 feet above the world now, I very nearly ignored what Catalina was trying to tell me. The horse, suspended out in the darkness, attached to the cliff face like an astronaut tethered to an errant spacecraft, was facing *up* the mountain, not down. The boy had not been on his way to pick up his grandmother when the accident occurred. He was on his way back *with* his grandmother.

In my most desperate, merciless, booming voice, I yelled out: "MI*GUEL!*"

He was instantly between us, pressing his hat across his chest like a baseball umpire's padded vest. His expression was twisted with fear, a shattered windshield of guilt. Catalina seized and shook him, demanding the truth, even though she already understood it. And as he nodded, his breathing turned to tortured hoots of grief, she gathered him into her arms and they both began to cry. What else was there to do?

I sidled out to the edge of the cliff and peeked over. A lifeless dark stared back. The horse snorted in its sleep and flicked its tail. I thought back to when I first arrived, to the casual regard that I gave the pit below and I wondered now which pile of garbage was actually a human being, which colorful clump had once been a gentle, plump old granny hurled violently through space to the rocks below, her crackling scream fading like the wail of a ghost.

Without thinking, I rushed over to the truck bed, retrieved the flashlight, then returned. I clicked the light on, but nothing happened. I shook it, turned it over, opened it. No batteries. "Shit!" I yelled. I stood there, staring down into the dark, my head book-ended with mournful groans.

Then came the inevitable.

"Señor, you must help her!" Catalina pleaded. "She is old. She is . . ." The word she should have been grasping for was "dead." But she didn't say it. Instead she mumbled about the pain the poor woman must be experiencing, as if anyone, let alone an elderly woman, could survive such a fall. Miguel was pawing her, weeping with her. He appeared unable to decide whether to comfort or seek comfort.

I told her that I had no intention of climbing down that cliff face. I was a pilot, I said, not a mountaineer. "We've got to get to a phone and call the police or an ambulance." I said this while pointing off toward the lights of San Luis and realized instantly that I might well have been pointing at the moon.

Catalina reacted by covering her ears and groaning louder. "Abuelita," she cried. "Poor Abuelita . . ."

In the wake of this, I again said, "Shit!" Then I chanced another peek over the cliff. *Goodwill Ambassador*, I thought as if acknowledging a family curse.

"Get me the rope, Miguel," I said bitterly. They both stopped crying and looked at me. "It just better be as strong as this goddamn tree." They watched in awe as I looped the rope around the front bumper of the truck and knotted it. With a great flourish, Miguel tossed the excess over the edge, watching it unwind into the sea of pitch. It wasn't his ass after all.

I took a deep breath and then coiled the rope between my legs and around my bottom, into what I thought was the proper rappelling position—at least according to what I'd seen in movies. I tested the rope with a hard tug, then leaned back, ready to descend.

Miguel said, "Do you wish me to hold that, señor?" He was pointing at my ankle pouch. "No, I don't wish," I said and once again, the overwhelming thought occurred to me that something sinister was about to happen, that all was not as it seemed. Only this time, I didn't feel guilty about thinking it.

But before I could apply any action to my concerns, Catalina climbed over the guardrail and swept toward me. She whispered, "Thank you, señor."

"Don't thank me yet," I answered.

She was pressing toward me, as if she intended to give me a good shove if I showed the slightest change of mind. "Careful," I said, but she cut me off with a firm kiss to my lips.

"That is for your luck," she said.

I swallowed hard, unable to lose the brief taste of her mouth. "I don't need luck," I stuttered.

"Then you may trust me instead."

I could have stood there forever, trusting her forever, lost in her sweet crystal blue eyes, but Miguel—playing the part of the pesky little brother who refuses to make himself scarce—stepped up and thrust the flashlight into my chest. I tried to push it back, saying, "No, it doesn't work," when the ledge bracing my feet gave way.

I fell, sucked down by the vacuum of the pit, past the tree, past the horse. For an instance, I clawed desperately at the air, actually letting go of the rope to do so. That's when the slack tightened around my backside, realigning my testicles in a hammer shot of pain. Somehow, my free hand found the rope again and I settled into a slow twist. I looked up to see that I was now some twenty feet below where I had been a moment before, my body floating below the wide stream of the truck's headlights that painted the sky above. The dark shadow of the horse, sensing a disturbance, immediately began to shift. One of its legs kicked out rudely and it whinnied. And I thought, *Jesus, it's going to tumble over and take both of us down.* But Catalina's dark silhouette appeared above me. She made a shushing noise and the horse quieted. As I took stock of my situation, about whether to descend or not, I discovered that I still gripped the flashlight in one hand. I tried to slip it into my back pocket, but it fell and was quickly swallowed by the darkness. I didn't hear it hit. I imagined it striking the old woman on the head as she writhed below, still clinging to life, wondering what the hell could possibly be next?!

If there even *was* a grandmother, I thought, and I looked up.

Both Miguel and his sister were staring down at me. They seemed to be grinning nervously. Perhaps because I was still alive and I was helping them. But more likely, I thought with intense confidence, because they knew they had me. Some blessed humans have that innate ability to detect betrayal before it occurs. Others—the blissfully ignorant, the doubly blessed—are constantly betrayed without ever realizing it. An unfortunate few, however, are cursed to know they are being betrayed while it happens—but are helpless to do anything about it. I was, apparently, of the latter persuasion. I had been conned, mugged and worse. The crafty Argentines above me were going to cut the rope as soon as I'd descended a few more feet. And this wasn't your clever town square con. This was nothing short of brilliant. Complicated and dangerous, but brilliant. Concocted to sting me specifically? Or was it just opportunity? Set to catch the first mark to glide up that road. Who knew? I had a Rolex, fifty bucks and a credit card. A treasure to the woman and boy above me.

I wondered then if there were some way I could turn the tables, get myself out of this mess. But then Catalina called out to me: "Is everything alright down there?" This was followed by Miguel's suppressed laughter and robust snort from the horse. That's when I realized that they couldn't see me, hanging just below them in the dark.

"Shut up!" She whispered harshly to her brother, then told him to get something. My mind filled in the missing word, *cuchillo*. Knife. Miguel's shadow disappeared. Catalina swept the frizzy hair from her eyes, all the while calling out, "Señor? You are all right? You have promise me, no? To help my poor abuelita, no?"

Another Spanish whisper from Catalina: "Give it to me! Hurry!" An awkward, fumbling silence. Then the sound of the knife blade—could one hear such things?—placed against the taut rope, resting against it, kissing it.

"Señor?" Catalina said.

And I found her unseeing eyes and I saw once again that she was beautiful and that she was innocent and that, in the blinding pain of the sudden descent, I had imagined it all. And I knew if I couldn't trust her—right then, at that precise moment in my existence, *her*—then I would never trust again. And what was the point of living without this small, but vital luxury? What was the point of living suspended, like the horse, knowing neither the thrill of rescue nor the relief of death?

And besides, all things considered, there really was nowhere else to go but straight down. Into the darkness. Into the ugly truth.

So that's exactly where I went.

STRONG ARM

"Henry J. Lippman!" a gruff, smoker's voice bellowed across the stretch of empty tables in the Iron Kettle Restaurant and Bar. "I'll be shot and stuffed if that ain't Henry J. Lippman!"

From the corner booth where a disinterested hostess had parked him moments before, Henry Lippman adjusted his glasses and searched for the source of the voice. He did not expect to recognize its owner since he knew very few people and was, after all, waiting for a woman. He certainly did not expect to see the tall, barrel-chested man threading his way between the tables, still laughing with amazement and familiarity.

With a nervousness that comes from knowing very few people, Henry fidgeted in his seat and began to fiddle with the buttons of his rumpled, rust-colored suit. On the table in front of him lay a vinyl photo album. He considered hiding it, but realized there wasn't enough time so he simply pulled it closer to his chest.

As the man drew closer, past the restroom entrance and a dartboard bristling with red and blue plastic darts, Henry could see the man's bulk was considerable and not a trick of early evening light. He wore a tweed sports coat over a polo shirt that was buttoned to the collar. A stylish mass of black hair framed a rigid, deeply tanned face. The man was carrying a manila folder. When he reached Henry's table he thrust out an enormous hand and said, "Henry, my main man . . . how in the hell are ya?"

Henry shook the man's hand and nodded dumbly. It was only after the stranger slid into the booth that Henry was absolutely certain the two had never crossed paths before.

"I'm waiting for someone," Henry said.

"You and me both, cowboy." The man glanced around and snapped his fingers into the air. "Service! Who do I have to see to get a little service around here?"

"Excuse me, but—"

"There she is!" the man said to the approaching waitress. He squinted in an effort to read her name tag and said, "Let's see, who do we have here? Judith. You don't mind if I call you Judy, do you? Judith sounds too old for a pretty young thing like you."

The waitress was smiling by the time she reached the table and clearly did not mind.

"Judy," the man said, pursing his lips in a contemplative manner. "My good friend and I are suffering from a serious lack of spirits, to the extent that we have outright forgotten the meaning of a good tip. Can you help a couple of poor patrons get their memory back?"

The waitress crossed her arms and frowned, hamming it up. "Well, I can sure give it the ol' high school try," she said.

"That's my girl. What's your poison, Hank?"

"Listen," Henry said, "I really think—"

"Wait, don't tell me." The man shut his eyes and pressed his fingers into the base of his tanned scalp before exclaiming, "Long Island Iced Tea! Am I right?"

"I don't—"

"Let's make it two, Judy. And be a peach and go real easy on the teasy."

The stranger examined the waitress's rear as she turned to walk off and for a moment, Henry thought the man might actually reach out and grab it. Instead, the man leaned back and smacked his lips. "Now that's a fridge I'd love to raid at midnight, eh?"

"Look," Henry said. "You've got me mixed up with someone else. I don't know you. Now, please. I'm waiting for someone."

"Jesus, Mary, Joseph, brother," the man said. "You act like you're waiting for a movie star or something." He hooked his thumb back toward a flickering television set perched above the bar. "You'd think Lisa Williams herself was going to get up from behind the news desk, walk right out of the screen and plop down in this booth with you."

Henry started to speak, but stopped. He stared across the table at the man. "Who are you?" he said.

"Who am I, who am I," the man muttered. "Who's anybody in this crazy make-believe world, huh?"

The waitress reappeared carrying a tray with two drinks. The man winked at her as she set the drinks down. "Careful now," he said, patting the manila folder. "Top secret documents."

"Who the hell are you?" Henry repeated after the waitress had gone.

The man carefully removed the straw from his drink, shook it beside the table, then tossed it behind the napkin dispenser. He positioned his drink in front of him, centering the glass on the coaster. "Name's Carl, Hank," he finally said. "You don't mind if I call you Hank, do you? Makes you seem smarter somehow."

"You're with the studio, aren't you?"

"You see? It's working already."

"Where's Lisa?" Henry said.

Carl sipped his drink and his eyes bulged in drunken affectation. "Good lord, that's what I call *easy* on the tea." He plucked a napkin from the dispenser, dabbed at the corners of his mouth, and said, "Relax, Hank. You look like you're about to climb out of that cheap suit. Let me eliminate the mystery right off the bat by telling you that Lisa Williams—kind-hearted celebrity that she is—will not be joining you this evening."

"I don't understand."

"Sure you do. You're no Bill Gates, but you're not brain dead either. I mean, what did you think? Lisa was going to drop everything and cancel the nightly news so she could go knock back a few beers with a perfect stranger?"

"But that's not true. You see—"

"I know, I know. You watch her every night, ten o'clock sharp. Never miss a broadcast. According to Nielson, that makes you and about eighty thousand others in the greater metropolitan area."

Henry looked down at his own drink, then back at the man. "What do you want from me?"

"*From* you? Not a thing," Carl said. "I'm just here to talk and share a drink. Hey, the studio's picking up the tab, right?"

"Fine," Henry said and began to slide out of the booth.

Carl kicked his leg out suddenly, planting a lizard skin boot onto the edge of the padded seat. "Slow down there, cowboy," he said firmly. "I didn't walk in here empty handed. In fact, I have something that's a lot more valuable than a dream date with Lisa Williams."

Henry settled reluctantly back into the booth. His eyes scanned the room. Except for a busboy bouncing from table to table, lighting the candle centerpieces, the place was deserted. After a moment, he murmured, "I'm not scared of you."

Carl stared straight back with an expression of mild contempt. The calm and even strength of his glare compelled Henry to look away, back down at the untouched drink.

"You have a drinking problem, Hank?" Carl said.

Henry scoffed. "Do I look like I have a drinking problem?"

"That's not always a factor."

"Well, I don't."

The faint thump of music emanated from a corner speaker nestled behind two large plant stands that were fashioned to look like tree stumps. The song was a light-hearted rap tune, totally inappropriate for the rustic atmosphere the restaurant seemed to be trying to cultivate.

Carl offered a raffish smile. "Listen to that, will ya? Some punk waiter probably plugged that into the sound system when the manager wasn't looking. I bet the kid's whiter than white and lives in a gated community uptown. In the Army, we used to call them wiggers."

"Is this what you want to talk about?"

"The thing is, it really doesn't matter how hard you try. On the outside, you are who you are and there's not much you can do to change it. The inside's a whole different story. What are you, Hank, about thirty?"

"I'm twenty-five."

Carl chuckled. "Right. Twenty-five. That's what I meant. All the more reason you shouldn't be so infatuated with a forty-plus year-old woman. You do know Lisa is over forty, right?"

"Of course I do."

"Oh, right. Dumb question. You probably even know her birthday."

"March 18."

"Fucking amazing. You should be on one of those trivia shows. One where all the categories are 'Lisa Williams'."

"I haven't done anything wrong."

"Who said you did? I'm just trying to figure out how a man like you—excuse me, a *young* man like you—can overlook such a big age gap."

"She's beautiful."

"Hey, no argument here. 'Course, the screen helps a little."

"Screen?"

"Oh, sure. They put a screen in front of the camera to soften up the skin, smooth out Mother Nature. Let's face it, a forty-something woman in show biz isn't exactly fighting off casting directors. Hell, *thirty* is considered long in the tooth, who's kidding who. And there's only so much a plastic surgeon can do."

Henry's eyes widened. "She's never had. . . ."

"Oh, sure she did, c'mon." Carl leaned forward, glanced side-to-side, then whispered conspiratorially, "I personally know of two trips she's made to Dr. Fix It, and the scuttlebutt says that number is short by half."

Henry looked down into his drink. He reached out and picked up the glass with both hands as if it were a small animal he intended to strangle. He raised the glass to his lips and took a long, deep drink. He grimaced and wiped his mouth with the back of his hand. "It's those goddamn producers," he said. "They're all jackals. They use you up and spit you out."

"I'm sensing hostility here, Hank."

"Stop calling me that."

"You ever watch Channel Nine?"

"What?"

"WMBL. Joyce Windham's the anchorwoman over there. Now there's a girl for you. Can't be more than twenty-one, twenty-two."

"No, you don't understand. I—"

"And those lips. Think about what she can do with those lips, heh?"

"That's not why I care about Lisa."

Carl laughed cheerlessly. "I know that, Hank. I'm just yanking your chain."

"You're confusing me."

"Funny, you don't sound confused. Neither do all those letters and cards you keep sending Lisa. Making all kinds of subtle demands. 'You *must* see me or else.' Serious stuff."

"There's nothing in my letters that suggests that I would ever want to . . . to . . ."

Carl raised his eyebrows. "To what?"

"That I would ever want to harm Lisa. I—"

"Harm?" Carl said. "Did you say 'harm'?" He rapped his knuckles on the table and deepened his voice. "Let the record show, ladies and gentlemen, that the first mention of harm came from the defendant, Hank Lippman."

"No, wait—"

But Carl was already laughing again. "I'm playing with you, Hank. Good lord, you're a serious duck. I know you don't want to harm her. Your letters didn't say a thing about that. If they had"— and here Carl's face took on a dark set—"if they *had*, you and I wouldn't be having this pleasant chat. You and I would be dancing in the street. Like the song says, right?"

"What's that supposed to mean?" Henry said.

Carl shrugged and took another sip of his drink. He reached out for the photo album. "Mind if I take a look?"

Henry pulled it back against his chest.

Carl gripped one corner of the album. He winked and drummed the fingers of his free hand on the manila folder. "C'mon, Hank . . . I'll show you mine if you show me yours."

Henry relaxed his hold and Carl pulled the album free. He set it atop the folder and grinned as if it were a meal he was planning to devour. After winking again at Henry, he flipped open the cover to reveal a neatly pressed spread of newspaper clippings of various sizes. The smallest proclaimed, *Local Teen Wins Beauty Contest*. Another announced the hiring of Lisa Williams at the television station while a more recent one hailed her receipt of a journalism award. The oldest article was also the largest and took up half a page. The yellowed clipping bore the headline, *Young Girl Helps Deliver Neighbor's Baby*. A black and white photo showed a girl in a hospital room, beaming with pride, holding up a newborn smothered in blankets. A picture of a ramshackle trailer home accompanied the article.

Carl scanned the clippings, his brows knitted up in an almost feral reflex of concentration.

"She was only ten years old when she delivered that baby," Henry said. "It's what got her interested in being a journalist."

"Looks like a wonderful neighborhood."

"She came from very humble beginnings."

"Fascinating," Carl said, although he was already turning the page.

"Of course, that was when her last name was Puska. She—"

"And what's this? High school photos?"

Henry nodded. "They're from her school yearbook. There's nothing illegal about that. Anyone can order a yearbook from anywhere."

"Oh, hey, I'm sure you're right about that, counselor."

"And that's her at college. She majored in journalism and graphic arts."

Carl flipped ahead to the last page. "Well, lookie here," he said. "A bona fide WBAL publicity shot."

"She even signed it. Look at the inscript—"

"She didn't sign it, Hank."

"Excuse me?"

"Lisa gets hundreds of these requests every month. Her assistant reads the fan letters and autopens all the publicity shots."

"I don't believe that."

"Sure you do." Carl closed up the album, leaned back and sighed. He took another sip of his drink. "Let me ask you something, Hank. Do you masturbate over these pictures?"

Henry snatched the album back. "That's sick."

"Oh, I know it's sick. I know it, but I've got to ask. You see, we had this guy last year who wasn't as biographically conscious as you. He was convinced that Lisa was speaking directly to him through the television every night. He claimed she was sending him secret messages that made him masturbate. He was pretty pissed about it. Wanted to kill her."

"I didn't know."

"Why would you? Not something the studio wants on the front page. Goes with the territory though. Every anchor woman in the country's got a dozen wackos spooging up their basement television screens. One or two of them are packing more than their dicks. Not that I'm complaining. Keeps me punching the clock."

"So you're some kind of bodyguard?"

"Me? A celebrity babysitter? Hell no. No, I'm what you might call a . . . a persuader. I help people look inside themselves. I help them decide things. Especially people who might otherwise have a difficult time making the right decision. Of course, I can't help people unless I understand them."

"I'm not crazy."

"And I'm not a shrink. Which leaves us with that." He pointed at the album. "And the letters."

Henry took another gulp of his drink and set the glass, mostly ice now, back on the table. He shivered in an effort to steel himself. "I don't write well, I know," he said finally. "I never was very good at it."

"You're no Shakespeare, I agree."

"And that's why it's so important that I *see* her. That I talk to her face-to-face. I need her to know that she holds the key to my future. Something like that's just too important *not* to do face-to-face. You can understand that, can't you?"

"Go on."

"You see, we came from similar backgrounds, but she took all the right steps. She's been a hero, a popular student, and now she's a famous T.V. personality. She knows where I went wrong. I can see it in her eyes. It's as if she sees all the mistakes I've made and wants to help me get back on track. She's the only one in the world who's capable of seeing the pure me."

"The *what*?"

"The pure me. Me before I started making mistakes. Me without scars. Me without sin. Me without—"

"Jesus," Carl said, his face becoming an event of amusement and disgust that he could no longer hold back. "Where the hell did you get this script? Stalkers-dot-com? I mean, c'mon, Hank."

"It's the truth, I swear it."

But Carl was already waving him off, having heard enough. "Let's talk about the truth then, since you brought it up. First of all, you're not twenty-five, Hank. You're thirty-two. Know how I know? Because I've got the file right here." Carl patted the folder again. "You grew up in a trailer on the south side. Your mom's an alkie-slash-heroin addict who did a couple of stretches for solicitation, drug possession. Current whereabouts unknown. And as far as mistakes. I don't see a few of them in here, Hank. I see a *lifetime's* worth. I see multiple drunk and disorderlies, grand larceny, criminal trespassing, possession of stolen property three times over. Between juvie and the slam, that's a dozen years of seeing the world through a set of iron bars. You're what they call a petty criminal. You know what 'petty' means, Hank? It's a nice way of saying you're not that good. Kind of like 'husky' instead of fat. I don't have to tell you that the commandos pick up on that pretty quick in the dog house."

"Stop," Henry said softly.

"In fact, my sources tell me you spent a good deal of time biting prison pillows. That's one place where it doesn't pay to be popular, eh Hank? What's the going rate for a cell bitch these days? A few bucks? A few smokes?"

"Stop it!" Henry yelled.

The hostess was seating a table of four some distance away and glanced over in their direction. Henry covered his mouth nervously and coughed.

Carl sighed. "I'm not going to sit here and lie to you. I'm not going to tell you that I know how you feel, because I don't. I'm not like you at all. But I believe in the human spirit, Hank. I believe that you can make a better life for yourself. Tonight—to put it oh so simply—can be the first night of the rest of your life."

"You sound like . . ." Henry said, then faltered.

"Who?"

"Nobody."

"C'mon, who do I sound like?" For the first time since he sat down, Carl appeared offended and impatient. "Tell me."

"My parole officer," Henry said, trying to smile.

"Funny you should mention him," Carl snapped back. "Because I've got his name and number right here. How do you think he'd react to all those letters? You think he'd get misty-eyed?"

"Okay, okay," Henry mumbled, his voice beginning to crack.

"Or, I don't know, maybe he isn't the sentimental type. Maybe he'll just cuff your sorry ass and send you back to the Grey Bar Hotel. Where all your buddies are waiting. All those inked-up, jacked-up mother fuckers lining up to get at you—"

"Stop, please." Henry dropped his face into the crook of his arm and began to weep. His shoulders shook as he tried, in vain, to control himself.

Carl's voice softened as he reached out and squeezed Henry's elbow. "Hank—*Henry*—I'm on your side in this thing. I really am. I've got a job to do, sure. But that doesn't mean I want to see you get hurt."

"You don't know anything about me," Henry said, raising his head. Behind his glasses, now crooked on his face, his eyes had gone red in the sudden flood of tears and his cheeks were pink and glazed. He pointed at the folder. "You think that's me, but it's not. I wasn't always like this. Someone like you could never understand what I want."

"I might not understand what you want, but I know what you need. And as for this file." Carl's gaze dropped to the folder and, as if it held a reward he had been withholding for too long, slid it across the table to Henry. "It *does* tell your story, Henry. To a T. Don't believe me? Take a look. Go on."

Henry sniffled and wiped his nose with the sleeve of his suit. Warily, as if to test its temperature, he laid his hand on the folder. When he pulled back the cover, a stark white sheet of paper stared back at him. He pushed aside the top few sheets and found a dozen more beneath. All of them were blank.

"Nobody's ever going to save you, Henry," Carl said solemnly. "Not me. Not God. And for sure not Lisa Williams. You alone have the power to save yourself and rewrite your future. Are you willing to try?"

Henry closed his eyes and nodded.

"Good."

"But . . ." Henry said.

The glimmer of the impatience rolled across Carl's face. He shook off the expression with a strained, but sympathetic smile. "Go on," he said. "Don't be afraid. Say it."

"If you really wanted to help me—if you really understood what I need—you'd let me see Lisa." As the name left his mouth, Henry braced himself as if readying for a violent reaction from Carl.

But Carl did not even blink. His expression of pity and warmth and sympathy held steady. After a moment, he said, "Do you believe in fate, Henry?"

"Yes," Henry said. "Very much."

"I do too."

"You?"

"I'll prove it to you." Carl jumped up from the seat, reached over and plucked a dart from the dartboard behind the booth. He took three measured steps backward, deftly dodging a busboy on the way to the kitchen. He held the dart up vertically and said, "If I put this spike in the red, you forget about Lisa Williams and get on with your life. You stay out of jail. You embrace success and rewrite your future starting tonight. But if I miss, I'll admit I was wrong and walk out of here, no questions asked. I'll go back to the studio and let everyone know that Henry J. Lippman is a stand-up guy. Hell, I'll even see if I can get you on the set."

"That's not fate," Henry said. "That's luck. They're not the same thing."

"They're the same thing tonight, Henry. So what do you say? A bright future or the foxiest over-forty anchor woman in the city. You can't lose on this one."

Henry started to speak, then simply nodded.

Carl smiled. He squared himself with the dartboard and narrowed his eyes at it. In a graceful, fluid movement, he drew his arm back and threw the dart. It sailed through the air at a slight arch and thudded neatly into the tiny red bulls-eye.

Henry sat there staring at the dartboard, his mouth agape. Carl sauntered back to the table, picked up his drink and sipped it, then placed the half-full glass down in front of Henry. He said, "Battalion Dartboard Champion. Fort Campbell, Kentucky. Two years running. Sorry I didn't mention that before I tossed. So we have a deal, don't we Hank? Sure we do." He dug into his inside jacket pocket and retrieved a money clip. He peeled off a few bills and let them flutter to the table. "Here's a couple of Jacksons to keep your spirits up. Enjoy yourself. Then go home and go to sleep."

Henry's face was breaking apart again. He was looking around the table as if for something to hold onto. "But—"

Carl put his hand on Henry's shoulder and slid it up to the base of his neck. "Go home, go to sleep and forget about her."

"I can't," Henry said, tearing up again.

"You can, Hank. You can and you will. Because if you don't—" Carl's strong fingers bit down into Henry's shoulder "—if you *don't*—I'm going to seriously fuck up your world. I'm going to get a couple of my buddies with a flair for knee-capping and we're all going to do a little dancing in the street." Carl released Henry and stepped back. "Just like the song says."

After a quick adjustment of his jacket, Carl turned and walked away. He shared a laugh with the hostess and even gave her a kiss on the cheek before disappearing through the front door.

Henry's bottom lip quivered as he pushed up his glasses and wiped at his eyes with a napkin. The music from the speaker—this time a popular country tune—grew louder and drifted up and around him. A rowdy group of men in cowboy hats had assembled at the bar. One of them proposed a toast and they all raised their glasses with a hearty "Damn straight!"

Henry took a drink from Carl's glass. He looked at the folder for a moment then pushed it aside. He opened the photo album to the clippings. His eyes settled onto the grainy photograph of the beaming girl holding up the baby.

"Now that's my kind of hero," the waitress said over his shoulder. She had walked up behind him silently. She wore a bright, toothy smile on her face, probably brought on by the money scattered on the table.

"What?" Henry said to her.

The waitress pointed at the album and read the clipping's headline, "Young Girl Helps Deliver Neighbor's Baby."

"Oh. Right."

"Takes a brave little girl to do something like that."

"It's what got her started in journalism."

"Who?"

"The girl."

"Hmmm," the waitress said, considering. "I would have thought she'd want to be a doctor after that. Or a mother."

"But look at her eyes," Henry said. "You can see it in her eyes. It's like she's saying—"

One of the foursome at the distant table signaled to the waitress.

"Hold that thought, honey," the waitress said, somewhat relieved, and hurried off.

Henry placed the tips of his fingers on the photo and muttered to himself: "It's like she's saying, 'You weren't always like this . . .'"

Then he smiled weakly, tracing his thumb around the infant's face, around his own face, and said in a faltering voice: "You were a baby once . . ."

SEVEN RIFLES AT DAWN

I noticed three disturbing elements in Captain Moore's appearance as he swept through the front flap of the operations tent. The first was that he was mentally unhinged and the second was that he was quite irritated. Neither of these surprised me greatly nor did they differ from the general demeanor of the thirty or so Air National Guardsmen that I supervised at the munitions dump. After all, who wouldn't be just a tad stir-crazy, having been ripped from civilian life as if by an alien mothership, off-loaded onto a western Kuwaiti airfield that would have taken a year of construction just to make desolate, deprived of sleep, soap and sex, all in preparation of whacking a dictator who probably should have been whacked fifteen years before? No, what made me uneasy was that this particular unhappy, insane man also happened to be armed with an M-16 rifle that he held braced across his flak vest, at the ready, his left hand poised atop the charging handle, his right index finger probing the trigger guard.

Had he been one of my young troops, I would have said something semi-clever to kill the tension, something like, "At ease, cowboy. Nobody here but us infidels." But the captain's eyes, partially shadowed under the brim of his Kevlar helmet, bore the look of a mad monk bent on religious persecution. Humor did not go over well with such people. You might as well foam at the mouth and shout, "Hail Satan!"

So I said to him, "Everything alright there, Captain?"

"No, sergeant," he responded in a dead, dry voice. "Everything is definitely not alright here." He adjusted his grip on the rifle and cleared his throat. The sound—feral and severe—put me helplessly in mind of a wild west villain. This was probably because I had just watched an old black and white Western on the Armed Forces Satellite Network the night before and the bad guy—dressed in black so no one would miss it—made his first appearance by thrusting himself through the swinging doors of the town saloon and glaring at everyone, his eyes probing the crowd for any signs of goodness like a predator zeroing in on the weak or elderly prey within the herd.

Like the good guy in that movie scene—and for that matter, like the bar keep, the piano player, the startled patrons and prostitutes—I just stood there and did not move. We were like this—the captain and me—for a good twenty seconds. Although my mind played out a melodramatic bad guy theme song, there was no sound except the drumming flap of the tent roof in the violent desert wind and the distant clink of utility lights strung through the ceiling braces. A sudden thought seized me and began to race through my mind. *Whatever you do, don't—repeat DON'T—look to the left of the captain, at the rack of M-16s. In fact, stop thinking about looking because if you don't—*

I looked. The captain followed my gaze. He turned back and cleared his throat again.

Here it comes, I thought ridiculously. *I'm lookin' for the sheriff*, he was about to say, with slow, menacing purpose. And I would answer—since I was the only one in the tent—*Then you're lookin' for me, greenhorn*. Or was it, *Stop lookin' then 'cause you done found him*? Or maybe—.

"What can you tell me," the captain said, "about Allah?"

I swallowed hard. "Would that be Allah, the God, sir?" I said.

"Yep. That's the one."

"Well, sir, other than the fact that he's a god, I guess I couldn't tell you that much. I'm Catholic myself. Well, not a die-hard Catholic. More like a Christmas Catholic. And maybe Easter. Not that I'm proud of that or anything—"

"I just want to know if you can spell his name, sergeant. Could you do that for me?"

"Spell his name, sir?"

"That's right."

"A-L-L-A-H. Like that, sir?"

I might as well have dictated the Da Vinci Code itself, because the tension in the captain's stance eased, the bulge in his eyes relaxed. He exhaled, shuffled forward and nearly collapsed into one of the folding chairs by my field desk.

He made a show of swiping a layer of dust from his camouflage pants and, in a weary tone, began to explain the reason for his visit and his declaration that things were not alright. He had just returned from a survey of our bomb load—over three hundred 500-pounders nestled out in one of the pads, waiting patiently for the war to begin—and to his dismay, he had come across a bomb upon which someone had written, *Fuck you, Alah!* As he described the spelling error, a bloodless satisfaction began to spread across his face and his grip on the M-16—now cutting across his lap— tightened. He said he appreciated the fact that we'd been working long hours ramping up to the war, but the potential fallout should a Kuwaiti soldier happen to see the bomb loaded on a jet was too much to overlook. "This is the kind of thing that gets people killed," he added, although I didn't fully understand how this could happen.

I told him that my policy was that none of my airmen were allowed to write on a bomb unless they had something pithy to say, like *If you can read this, you're dead.*

The captain smiled, unamused, and said, "That should make your job easier."

"My job, sir?"

The captain was already standing, reassuming his bad guy posture. "That's right, sergeant. Whoever wrote it obviously can't spell Allah. Find that guy," he said, "and you've found your outlaw."

Outlaw? I thought. *Did he just say outlaw?*

He walked to the door, took another look at the rack of rifles, then turned slowly. "I'll be back in the morning for a name."

"A name, sir?"

"A name, sergeant. Whoever did this is going to pay. The war's about to start any minute. We're here to drop bombs, not religious slurs. We're the good guys, don't forget."

After he'd disappeared under the tent flap, I replayed his words, hoping to decipher what it was exactly that he expected me to do. As the deputy flight commander, the captain had always struck me as slightly unknowing and reserved, his expertise more attuned to flight-line operations than bomb building. This was fine by me because he had, until tonight, generally stayed out of my hair. I probably should have pushed back a little, told him not to worry, that I'd handle it. But his words about war and religion and retribution faded like the memory of sleep, soap and sex, and were quickly replaced in my mind by the grim bad guy, sidling out of the saloon, his spurs clinking after him: *I'll be back at daybreak*, the bad guy said. *You better have your gun. Either way there's a-gonna be some shootin'.*

I emerged from the tent vestibule and into a windswept desert night. The sky above bristled with stars as bright as sword points. To my right was an enormous California structure the size of a circus tent, its windows blacked out with cardboard and duct-tape. Even so, I could hear my men jostling about inside, a television blaring the theme song from *Friends*. A single terrorist could bag the lot of them without much trouble, especially since my sentry—placed there because of his incompetence handling explosives—was probably asleep at his post, as if to demonstrate his incompetence handling awareness.

Stretching out to my left, glazed purple in generator lights, was a wasteland of sand and demons, interrupted only by an occasional explosive barrier. When the wind dropped to nothing, you could hear those demons slithering over the thin brush, rattling the stretches of razor wire that ringed our base camp. The sounds could have been Arab terrorists, packed to the gills with blocks of C-4, whispering under their breath "'Fuck Alah'? I show you 'Fuck Alah'!" The more likely source was a stray dog or two, scampering after scraps of MREs or the hides of desert hares stupid enough to venture out in the moonlight.

Stray dogs were a big problem because the American end of the base was located—much to the delight of our Kuwaiti hosts—amid several large garbage dumps. We were authorized to shoot them on sight—the dogs, not our Kuwaiti hosts—because most were rabid. More than one of my airmen had expressed an eagerness to carry out the order, if only to vent their pent-up frustration. But the dogs—even the rabid ones—had so far proved smarter than us.

I happened to be a dog person myself, even a mangy mutt person, and didn't think I could shoot one. I had just such a dog when I was a kid. Cracker Jack was his name. Pancaked by a semi on Route 80 out of Ellicott City, Maryland. As I stood there, enjoying the stillness of the gathering twilight, trying to recall more images of my pet dog, another thought rudely occurred to me. *Jack.* That was the name of the sheriff in the movie the night before. Sheriff Jack Redding, the good guy. He wore a pearl-white cowboy hat and a frilly western shirt that looked like he stole it from a bandleader. I tried, but couldn't remember much more, although I knew that the deck was stacked against him. I knew this because he had said so. "The deck's stacked against me," Sheriff Jack told his wise-cracking deputy sidekick. The sidekick didn't have long to live. Like mangy mutts, they were always the first to go.

A silent, squat figure emerged from the darkness beside me. I started clumsily and fumbled for my weapon. Lucky for me, the figure was just Tech Sergeant Palmer, a guardsman from Alabama who was unique among his fellow southerners in that he had no accent and no humor. Tonight, he looked haggard and evasive in the dim generator lights. But at least his M-16 was slung across his shoulder, its business end pointing into the sand. He stood there, nestled in a Gortex jacket and did not speak, probably sympathetic to the fact that he had surprised me. He was puffing on the runt of a Turkish cigarette which, for some reason, were all the rage for American smokers.

"How'd it go?" he finally asked.

"How'd what go?" I said, nonchalantly trying to re-shoulder the M-16 that was now tangled around my forearm.

"Your meeting with Captain Maniac. I saw him walk in. Looked like he was going to light the place up."

"Thanks for coming to the rescue."

Palmer grinned humorlessly and shrugged. "I promised my wife I wouldn't get killed unnecessarily. Getting shot by a nutcase on your own side definitely qualifies."

For some odd reason, I felt compelled to defend the captain, if only to allay my own fears. "What makes you think he's crazy?"

Palmer dragged deeply on the cigarette, then spit out pieces of tobacco. "He's got that look. You know what I mean."

I turned and surveyed a dust devil that spiraled lazily through a line of jeep bobtails and over the camp clearing. "I guess I don't," I said.

"Plus, he's too quiet. Never makes a sound when he moves."

"Neither do you. You scared the shit out of me a minute ago."

Palmer dropped the remains of the cigarette butt between his boots and stepped on it. "You're not scared of me now are you?"

"You're not pointing a gun at me."

He started to grunt—I suppose out of amusement—then stopped. "Jesus, he drew down on you? Are you serious?"

"Well," I said. "I guess not technically. Christ, who knows? Ever get the feeling you're in the middle of a movie? A not very good one where the plot is almost as bad as the acting?"

He nodded. "Like a porn movie."

"Wha—? No, man. I mean . . ."

Palmer reached out and patted me judiciously on the back, as if to warn me against saying anything else. "I think you need some time off, sarge."

I turned in an attempt to explain, but stopped when I saw that Palmer was looking up at the stars. He wasn't being rude. He just didn't need to enable me to be anything other than dead serious. It was his way of doing me a favor. Sparing him my melodramatic interpretation, I laid out the captain's complaint and suggested we'd better check out the bomb pad to see if there was any truth behind it.

"Hell of a way to start the shift," he said.

"Hell of a way to start the war," I said.

We climbed into one of the jeeps and headed out to Pad Five, out to where we stored a dangerous gaggle of bombs destined for the second and third attack waves (the first wave being hooked up to every available jet on the base). The ten-minute drive took us past Bravo sector which had been cordoned off for a contingent of the Royal Air Force. The Brits weren't too keen on this arrangement—given that Bravo sector trended toward the base perimeter and so was more vulnerable to attack. To make matters worse, security for the fence line was the sole responsibility of the Kuwaiti Special Forces which had accomplished the difficult feat of earning unanimous contempt among all the Western allies on base. The joke was that if Iraqi sympathizers tried to bum-rush the dump, we were not to shoot the first screaming Arabs over the fence because those would be the Kuwaiti Special Forces retreating. From what I saw of them—mostly lightly armed relief sentries shambling along the perimeter road—the derision was misplaced. In fact, the Kuwaitis always looked roused and eager and battle-tested, unsupported as they were outside the wire.

Halfway to Pad Five, Palmer finally broke the silence, reiterating his lack of appetite for the captain's concerns. "Every bomb out there has something offensive written on it," he said. "That's the whole point."

"The thing is, he's coming back," I said. Helplessly, as if programmed, I added, "At dawn."

"What for?"

"To see if we found out who did it, I guess."

"So what if we do? What's he going to do, shoot the guy?"

As I angled the jeep down the side dirt road toward a distant constellation of generator lights, a pack of fleshless dogs crossed the road, a vision of hair and eyes and teeth slipping through the headlights, swallowed up by the darkness. I jumped at the sight of them although it probably wasn't noticeable the way the jeep was rocking. Palmer fashioned his hand into a pistol and made like he was shooting at them.

Like renegades, I thought, my eyes searching for the dogs in the black desert night. Like cattle thieves raiding the herd. Just like in the movie the night before. In fact, that's why the townsfolk hired Sheriff Jack in the first place. To catch and hang the cattle thieves. Not that the thieves would be easy pickings. They had a bad guy of their own. Only it wasn't quite as simple as that. No, because there was a woman involved. But that part was fuzzy, just like the ending. How *did* it end? I thought. I had watched the whole thing, from start to finish, the starchy morning sun seeping through the morale tent windows, a rowdy game of ping pong behind me. I had stared at the screen and watched the bad acting and heard the corny lines and even recall the closing credits. Why couldn't I remember the details? Why was everything, beyond good vs. evil, so dim? As if the plot, simple and dry as it was, had come unspooled in my mind, like a fuzzy childhood memory perched on the edge of recall?

"Who's Jack?" Palmer said.

"Huh?"

"You just said 'Jack.'"

"Did I?"

After parking the jeep at the entrance of Pad Five, we made our way through an opening at one corner of the ponderous berms and into a dead sea of bombs, some loaded and ready on flightline trailers, but most stacked on ground dunnage. It looked like a graveyard for giant cucumbers. I shone my flashlight over each bomb nose, chuckling as I went. As Palmer had said, just about every other bomb had something written on it and it wasn't long before I had identified several misspellings, although most were intentional as in, *Say halo to my leetle friend.*

Another read, *Don't you wish you fucked with the French?* Shouldn't it be *had* fucked with the French? I thought.

After a few passes through the maze, I was about to shrug the whole thing off and make up a lame excuse for the captain when Palmer whistled from the far corner of the pad.

"Found the guilty party," Palmer said as I approached. He shone his penlight down on the nose of the bomb. Sure enough, *Fuck you Alah* it read. The poet had used a silver magic marker that shimmered in the penlight. The script was small, angry and juvenile. Considering that most of my troops were angry juveniles, this did nothing to narrow the field of suspects.

"Betcha it's Harrison," Palmer said, leaning back against a nearby generator unit. In spite of the fact that the machine behind him was humming and stank of kerosene amid a field of high explosives, Palmer calmly lit up a Turkish cigarette. There was no one around to protest except me and he knew I wasn't in the mood.

"The part-time preacher?" I said. "Can you see that guy writing 'fuck'?"

"My priest back home can cuss the mud off a fence post." He looked up at the sky and considered, a lazy vine of white smoke gathering above his helmet, then said, "What about Wiley?"

"Wiley, Wiley," I said. "The senior airman with the lisp?"

"No, you're thinking of *Reilly*. I'm talking about the kid with all the acne. And attitude."

"What makes you think it's him?"

Palmer shrugged. "He's a kid. With attitude."

The enormous circular light perched atop the generator coughed, as if from Palmer's cigarette smoke. Wiry desert insects buzzed and tapped its glass face. The wind kicked up again, sending a pale plume of dust racing across the bomb pad like a terrified ghost.

We stood there, at a loss as to our next move. I finally rapped my fingers on the bomb and said, "Well, I guess we better go tell the guys. See if somebody confesses."

"And if somebody does?"

"What else can I do?" I said. "I'll have to shoot him."

"Or her," Palmer said. "Don't forget, we've got one woman."

"Or *her*," I said, irritated that he wouldn't credit me one dumb joke.

I started back toward the jeep, but lingered when I noticed Palmer wasn't following. I turned. He was staring out over the sea of bombs, his eyes glassy and tired.

He drew heavily on his cigarette and said, "Makes you think, doesn't it?"

"What?"

He made a sweeping, almost dismissive gesture at the bombs. "The shit we're fixing to step on."

"Does it bother you?

"What?"

"This," I said, making the same sweeping gesture. "You don't exactly strike me as a guy who would go for all this war stuff."

"I'm here, right?" He dropped the butt and stamped it into the pad gravel, another major violation of explosive etiquette. "Besides, they've got it coming, I guess."

I looked out over the bombs. "They better."

Palmer held the door open for me as I stumbled across the raised threshold of the California. Once inside, the warmth and bestial smell of body odor—as shameless as a gymnasium—hit me full in the face and I winced, muttering "Good *God!*" If I expected recognition for my less than grand entrance I was disappointed. Throughout the room—which was no bigger than a three-car garage—and in various degrees of age and undress, were thirty or so men and one woman. Most were decked out in desert camouflage that shimmered in the overhead florescent lights. A large screen television blared from one corner—a war movie this time—although no one seemed to be paying attention to it. An excess of makeshift furniture and cots cluttered the room, as randomly arranged as pick-up sticks. Wooden, pew-like benches, stacked with chemical warfare gear and helmets, spanned the full length of each wall.

I stood there and watched for a moment, fully understanding the reason no one acknowledged me. My presence usually equaled bad news. I was the guy who made them lift heavy things and shuttle high explosives up and down rutty gravel roads. Some of the men I knew personally, but the balance came from a mix of other units across the country. Alabama, New Mexico, Colorado and even a couple of fine representatives from the island territory of Puerto Rico. Back home, they were cops, prison guards, college students, unemployed drunks, fresh-faced killers. One guy was plucking a nylon string guitar. Another two—both armored up in Kevlar vests and sitting on empty 20-millimeter ammo cans— were engaged in a quiet game of Go. Still another lay stretched out and snoring in the corner, his helmet covering his face. The only woman on my shift—a middle-aged staff sergeant named Regina Potts—was hunkered down in a camp chair, twisting her hair up in a bow as if girding herself for battle. Her voice was also the only one I heard upon entering. She was complaining bitterly to an uninterested airman beside her that her ex didn't have the balls to go through with it—whatever "it" was.

We were the Air Guard, which meant that we were, all of us, extremely likely to survive the war. We wouldn't be on the front lines, after all. But still, I had the incredible sense, a sickly and forever sense, that we were not all going home.

A pair of F-16s ripped through the sky above the ceiling. All sound within the California, save for the thunderous roar of afterburners, evaporated. Nobody in the room even flinched or made an effort to cover their ears, the deafening sound being so common, the damage to ear drums long since accepted.

When the sound finally faded, I listened, suddenly resolved not to allow the image of anything western from creeping into my mind. But no sooner had I made this commitment than another bleary scene from the movie clobbered me with typhoon force. The distant F-16s became the crackle of campfires on a windswept prairie. The airmen before me became a huddled and imposing posse of killers, their murmuring conversations clipped and wrought with purpose. Snips of voices surfaced and rang in my ear, each with some vague hint of tin-horn language found only on a Hollywood movie script.

"Don't forget," one was saying in answer to a question. "We're on the eve of war." And the answer: "We've been on the 'eve' of war since we got here. If this eve lasts any longer, I'm going to break out my six-guns and burn down Dodge!"

"It don't matter how good looking she is," another voice said in a consoling manner, "some cowboy somewhere is tired of her shit."

Far off, the peaceful game of Go took an unstable turn. "Check the rulebook then if that'll make you happy. But don't tell me that's how you play back home 'cuz you ain't home. You're in the wild fucking west!"

And a firm woman's voice—the lone woman's voice: "So I told my mom, if that sonuvabitch wants the kids so bad, he can have 'em! Let him ride in that crazy rodeo 24/7 and see how he likes it."

I turned to Palmer, flashing a goofy grin of amazement, expecting him to have the same befuddled reaction to what I was hearing. But his eyes were bloodshot and serious, no time for levity.

The thought of introducing the captain's paranoia to the scene was suddenly nauseating. I was about to wave Palmer off, to leave my troops to their calm before the storm. But he interrupted this thought by barking across the room: "Ears up, people!"

It took only a second to realize that Palmer wasn't setting me up for a speech. Instead, he was pointing at the television screen. The war movie had disappeared and in its place was what looked like the glowing embers of a campfire, but was in fact the silhouette of a city beneath which read the caption: *CNN Breaking News—Baghdad Is Burning!*

The room turned still and quiet except for a collective shift as if everyone was craning toward the television. The screen split in two, one focusing on a fiery city of mayhem and the other on a lone reporter standing on a rooftop, shouting into a microphone and looking ridiculous in an oversized green helmet and flak vest. With his free hand, the reporter gripped the top of his helmet as if he thought a strong wind might shear it off his head. The delayed feed made his dialogue with an unseen anchorman difficult to follow, but the gist of the conversation seemed to be a statement put out by something called (or at least translated into) the Iraqi Information Service, claiming that the U.S. Air Force had destroyed three hospitals and a retirement home in the first sortie.

"Hell," one of my men said from the corner, "why not throw in a day care center and make it a hat trick?"

"Because it's not daytime, dumb ass," his buddy said.

"Who the hell believes this shit is my point."

"Who do you think?"

"I'm asking."

"I thought you were being rhetorical."

"Well, I'm not."

"So where does that leave us?"

"Will you guys shut up!" Regina said, like a mother shushing her unruly kids.

A few men in the room turned and looked over at me. They were no longer the ragged ruffians of just moments before, their faces leathered and red, their eyes hard and keen. Now I was looking straight into the eyes of cattle. Cattle lost on the prairie, surrounded by rustlers. Cattle demanding answers and attention to their plight. *So how about it, sarge?* the eyes demanded. *How about rounding us up and leading us home?*

I nudged Palmer with my elbow and the two of us pushed back outside and under the dark awning of the California. "I'm heading over to HQ," I told him. "Have everyone sit tight, and I'll let you know what's up."

Palmer nodded. "You want me to send out a posse?"

I started to speak, but stopped. "A *what?*"

"Patrol, sarge. A patrol. Do you want me to send one out to check the perimeter? We're probably in Delta by now."

I nodded. Palmer spit into the sand. "What about the other thing?" he said. "You want me to assign somebody to paint out the bomb noses?"

I sighed and fished the jeep keys from my fatigue pocket. I thought about the captain. I thought about Sheriff Jack. I said, "Hang 'em."

"What?"

"Jesus. I mean, paint 'em. *It.* Paint it."

Palmer eyed me suspiciously, then spit again. "He's not going to like it."

"Who?"

"The guy I tell to paint the bomb. Especially since we're going to drop it soon."

"Yeah, well . . ." I said, looking at my watch, surprised to see that we were only a couple hours from dawn. "We just need to be ready."

"For the captain," Palmer said, his voice now rich with melodrama although I couldn't quite tell whether it was sarcastic too.

I tried to laugh, but Palmer only shook his head. "You okay there, sarge?" he said, slapping me on the shoulder, a father bucking up a son on the eve of his first T-ball game. "You still think everything's a porn movie?"

"Right," I said. "Sure."

"What the hell? I'll grab a few of the guys, too. Get them rifled up." He paused. "Just in case there's a showdown."

"At dawn," I said.

Palmer grinned and gestured over his shoulder, out into the desert where we could hear the distant but furious whine of jet engines running through their take-off checklists. "Like everything else."

I didn't need CNN to tell me that the war started. Inside the Vault—as we called the locked-down, sandbagged bunker that served as the squadron headquarters—a mass of officers in flight suits whirled around with energy and excitement, each as clumsy in their movements on the ground as they were undoubtedly graceful in the air. I usually stopped by at the start of each shift, to pick up flying schedules, build sheets, roster reports. Every time, I had seen only serious and glum faces, going about the cold business of war planning, like God deciding where the next earthquake or tsunami would strike.

But not any more. Now they were alive and firing on all cylinders. Scooting from one end of the cluttered room to the other, radios clacking, control boards blinking. It looked like the stock exchange on a good day.

I located my commander—a light colonel in wrinkled fatigues and a crop of fine, blond hair—huddled in the corner with several other officers. Compared to the rest of the room, they appeared rapt and useless, like debris that had been driven hard into the nook by the powerful force of a flood.

After dodging several pilots and aides, I reached the corner of the room and adjusted myself in a way I hoped would indicate impatience. My ears honed in on the colonel's voice, expecting to hear calm commands. Instead, I found him in the midst of a joke: "So the information minister calls Saddam's body doubles into a bunker," my commander said, eyes animated with his own knowledge of the punch line, "and he tells them, 'Boys, I've got good news and bad news. The good news is that Saddam survived the bombing so you guys still have a job. The bad news is he lost an arm!'"

Amid the chalky eruption of laughter that followed, I cleared my throat, then glanced sideways. Through an arched doorway was a darkened room where several pilots were gesturing enthusiastically at a large-screen television. The screen displayed the grainy videos of a recent bomb run. By their expressions, I could see they were happy with the mission. They nodded frequently and, at one point, as the center of the screen flashed white in a terrific explosion, they pumped their fists, murmuring hearty congratulations all around.

To my left sat a young two-striper at an olive drab field desk, staring into a humming laptop computer. The screen displayed a news website with screaming black letters that read: *U.S. TO IRAQ: NO MORE MR. NICE GUY!*

And just then—probably because I was focusing on every glowing screen in the bunker—another rush of the Western movie plot swept over me again. The sheriff had indeed been the hero, sent in to the sparsely populated county to confront a gang of cutthroat rustlers who had been terrorizing the only town. The townsmen, in fact, had strung up one of the rustlers and, of course, that didn't sit well with the other rustlers who, it turns out, were all related to the hung man. They were also united in their commitment to burn down the town. So the hero—Sheriff Jack—was sent in to . . . to what? Shoot the rustlers? Or maybe to protect them from getting shot by the townsmen? And here my memory started to blur again and I couldn't quite remember. I knew there had been a shoot-out because at some point, the bad guy had been hired. Hired to kill the sheriff. Except that the side-kick got it first. Then the sheriff got mad—hey, who wouldn't? That's when the showdown was set. For dawn. Except that the woman—the love interest of the sheriff—was also the love interest of the bad guy. Or was it the side-kick? There had to be—

"Sergeant!" my commander yelled. He was standing right in front of me, straining to make up the six-inch difference in our heights. He waved his open hand in front of my eyes as if testing my vision. "You with us this morning?"

"Yes, sir," I said. "Absolutely."

Before I could say anything else, the colonel's face turned grave and he let spill the low-down. The meaty need-to-know stuff. Life as we knew it—twelve-hour shifts of waiting around for the first go—was now over. Now would come the real work. The war work. Building bombs around the clock—high drag, low drag, bunker busters, ground-burst, air-burst, no-burst, you name 'em—staying four or five missions ahead. No time to write pithy comments. We'd barely have time to fuse and wire them before they'd be strapped up on the 16s and whisked away like the mail man bringing bad news.

He handed me a thick folder of paperwork that I was supposed to relay to my shift replacement. I tucked the folder under my arm and coughed into my hand. "There's something I need to talk to you about, sir. Actually it's more of a someone than a something."

"Yes?" I could tell he was impatient. He had already positioned his body to perform an about-face.

"It's about Captain Moore. I think there may be a problem." And here I got the sudden sense that Captain Moore himself was standing right behind me, so much so that I turned with a start only to find the room still alive and uninterested in my existence or fears or imaginary wild west world.

When I turned back, I found that the colonel was also glancing around the room, muttering "Captain Moore, Captain Moore . . ." until an irritated expression worked over his features and seemed to snap his mouth shut. Then he narrowed his eyes at me and said, "I haven't seen him in a while. He told me he was going out to survey the bomb load."

"Yes, sir. And he did that. The thing is he struck me as a little . . . unstable."

"What do you mean by 'unstable'?"

"Well, sir . . ." I said, and the "sir" hung between us like a bad smell. And as I spoke, blundering through my concerns about Moore's accusations and warning, my commander—the man charged with my safety and the safety of my men—kept fixed upon me an unsympathetic, unblinking gaze. Through it all, the bad smell gradually took on the defining characteristics of a prairie—wet grass, rotted fernwood, and cow shit—and completely engulfed me. The bustle of war plans, cackle of radios and ringing phones turned into the clop of hoofs and the rattle of wagon wheels creaking through the sloppy mud streets of a western town.

Finally, as if he had heard all that I had to say before, my commander smiled, shook his head and said in a voice louder than I would have preferred. "And you're worried he's gone off the deep end. Is that it? Is that the bottom line?"

"I'm just worried he may be . . ."

Again, the colonel cut me off. "What, sergeant? Dangerous?" He reached out and laid a firm hand on my shoulder, again trying to raise up on his toes to gain some height. "Captain Moore is just dog tired, sergeant," the colonel said. "And like everybody else right now . . . including you . . . he's about to be a little preoccupied with killing the enemy to waste any time killing his own men."

At that precise moment, as if on cue, the airman seated in front of the laptop let out a whoop. "Goddamn army!" he shouted. The bold headline lighting up the laptop screen included the CNN logo and the words: RAMPAGING U.S. SOLDIER KILLS OWN MEN WITH GRENADE!

The airman was scrolling down the page when he looked up and blinked his eyes, as if surprised to find the colonel and me standing there. He was chewing on a drinking straw. "Goddamn army," he said with an embarrassed grin.

I looked down at the commander's hand on my shoulder. He took it away as though shying away from heat. Then he said, "You're not having doubts, are you, sergeant?"

"Sir?" I was still looking at my shoulder, where his hand had been. I was beginning to get annoyed, something he obviously mistook for doubt.

"About the war. About what we need to do."

"If I had any doubts, sir, I wouldn't be worried about the captain. I'd be worried about myself."

"I'm not sure what that means, sergeant, but I'm relieved to hear it."

When I finally looked into his eyes, I found myself staring not at the face of my commander, but rather at the saddle-bag leathery features of a wise old ranch hand. And even though I knew the commander's lips said, "Don't worry, sergeant. Captain Moore's one of the good guys," the words that I heard had the unmistakable hint of West Texas drawl.

He's a-coming for you, Sheriff, the drawl said. *He's madder 'n a stuck bull and twice as mean and he aims to kill you. You and anybody that gets in his way . . .*

My mind was still on the movie—where else?—when I stopped in at the munitions security gate, gently navigating the concrete barriers that would, I suppose, prove a slight nuisance to the next suicide trucker barreling through, screaming *God is Great!* My sentry hopped up from a sandbag lounge seat he had created near the guard shack. He had been sleeping. I could tell from his droopy eyes and slouched shoulders that looked as if an invisible anvil were strapped to his back. He smacked his lips to keep from yawning, shined his flashlight into my face, then asked to see my ID.

I squinted back at him. "Don't I remind you of somebody you know?"

He cleared his throat and turned off the flashlight. "You said I should check everybody's ID, right? Especially now that the war's started."

"Do you honestly believe," I said, "that I meant other Americans? Other Americans you know and recognize?"

I gunned the engine and started to drive off. My foot quickly came down on the brake. A surge of guilt—the guilt of being wrong—swept through me, but before I could apologize to the sentry, something else occurred to me. "Do me a favor," I said to him. "If Captain Moore comes through, call me on the radio before you—"

"Too late."

"What?"

"Came through about a half hour ago."

My eyes darted around as if the captain were about to leap out of the desert brush and onto the hood of my jeep, firing off a clip from his M-16.

"He showed me his ID," the sentry said.

My next stop was Pad Five, looking for the captain's Humvee. It was nowhere in sight. The bombs were all trailerized and undisturbed, just as Palmer and I had left them. Generators buzzed and silver shafts of lights crisscrossed each other, gleaming off the cold metal bomb bodies, casting grotesque shadows unto the hastily constructed berms. I thought about getting out to examine the bombs more closely, to see if the nose of one bomb in particular had been painted out, but instead wheeled around and drove off toward base camp.

As I pulled into the open clearing in front of the operations tent, I scanned the area, seeing only familiar and torn-up jeep bobtails. No Humvee. No captain.

I sat there a moment, the jeep idling, wondering where he could possibly be and whether he would emerge from the shadows like that wild west villain. It occurred to me then, watching another burst of aircraft thunder through the sky above, that daylight would soon be upon us. The night sky was, in fact, fading quickly, exposing the pock-mocked desert terrain that resembled burnt skin.

That's when I remembered the sheriff, clearly, opening the chamber of his six-gun right before the climactic scene. He made sure the gun was loaded, then spun the chamber so that it buzzed, then snapped it shut with flick of his wrist. I looked down at my

M-16 in the seat beside me. I took hold of it, snapped back the charging handle to chamber a round, then clicked the safety off. I had to be ready, I decided. For anything.

I got out of the jeep and made my way through the vestibule of the operations tent. Once out of the wind, I heard a slight rustle just past the interior door. As I began to part the canvas flap, I could actually hear bones and joints stiffen on the other side. Inside, grouped in a football huddle and taking no notice of me at all, were Palmer and two of my airmen. They were whispering at each other angrily.

"What the hell's going on?" I said, and the small huddle of people exploded outward, each of them jumping off the floor in a panic, swinging their guns around aimlessly. I shut my eyes and grimaced, more to keep from pulling the trigger of my M-16 than any real fear I would be shot.

When I opened my eyes, Palmer was waving the others back with one hand and ranging me down the sights of his 9-millimeter pistol with the other. "Sweet jumpin' Jesus!" he shouted at me, eyes bulging.

As I took in the scene, I realized that one of the two airmen was our token female, SSgt. Regina Potts. She was gritting her teeth and cursing, thrusting the business end of her rifle toward the earth as if she regretted not using it.

"Sorry, sarge," Palmer said, reholstering his 9 mil. "Thought you were the captain," he said.

"Has he been here?"

Palmer turned to the young airman—the same one who had been playing Go earlier and said, "Tell the sarge what happened."

"Well," the airmen said sheepishly. "I went out to spray paint the bombs like Sergeant Palmer said . . ."

"Which is a bunch of bullshit," Regina snapped.

I ignored her. The airman continued, describing to me how he had gone out to Pad Five with a can of spray paint. There,

Captain Moore overtook him. But before the two could speak, a stray dog approached from out of the darkness. The captain responded to the animal's appearance by crouching down and coaxing it closer, snapping his fingers as if offering a treat.

"I told him not to do it," the airman said. "That the dog could be rabid. But he kept on snapping his fingers. And when the dog got close enough, Captain Moore reached out and grabbed it by the scruff of the neck. Then he whipped out his bayonet and sliced its throat. Right there in front of me. All the time, he stood there grinning and watching it squirm around on the ground, blood gushing everywhere."

"All for nothing, too" Regina said. "Some kind of goddamn officer!"

Palmer waved a hand at her outburst, and I got the impression that he had argued with her earlier. Regina responded by pacing along the line of plastic tent windows.

"After the dog stopped moving," the airman continued. "The captain picked it up and put into the back of his Humvee. Just as calm as can be. Like he was taking it home as a trophy."

"Did he threaten you in any way?" I said.

"I don't think so. Told me not to worry about the bomb. Told me it was too late."

"It was never too late!" Regina shouted.

Finally, I turned to her. "What the hell," I said, "is your problem?"

"Wait!" Palmer interrupted, gesturing toward the young airman. "Before we get into that, tell him the last thing the captain said. Go on."

The airman took a deep breath. "Right, well, I said to him, 'why didn't you just shoot it, captain?' And he said, get this, he said, 'I'm saving my bullets. For later.'"

"For dawn," I said.

"No," the airman said, somewhat puzzled. "He said 'For *later*.'"

"It gets better," Palmer said. He gestured toward Regina and she acknowledged him by grunting, as if she was no longer interested in speaking. She had stopped pacing and was standing there, feet planted shoulder-width apart, arms crossed, pursing her lips. I looked at her, then at Palmer. Palmer finally spoke up: "Regina was the one who wrote on the bomb."

"You?" I said. "Why would you write that?"

"I didn't," she snarled back at me. "Not that I give a rat's ass about Allah."

"Okay, okay," I said, "why don't we start from the beginning. Or just the part that makes sense."

Palmer started to speak, but Regina cut him off. "The beginning was when that sunuvabitch asked me to marry him.

"Who?"

"Alan."

"Who the hell is Alan?"

"Exactly," Palmer said.

I had the sudden and overwhelming sense that we had descended far beyond an old western, deep into a scene from *Abbot and Costello Meet Wyatt Earp*—if there was such a movie.

"Alan is my ex," Regina said. "The sunuvabitch. I wrote 'Fuck you, Alan' on the bomb. *Alan.* Maybe my handwriting was a little off, but it sure as hell wasn't Allah!"

"Exactly," Palmer said.

I felt sick with weariness. My gut clenched. I was about to remove my helmet and clear my rifle when I heard the undeniable scrape of a boot heel sounded outside on the floorboards of the tent vestibule. I swung around and raised my rifle. I could see the light of morning now seeping in from beneath the flap.

In fact, that light was the only difference between the captain walking into the tent and the bad guy villain thrusting himself into through the saloon doors. The captain took up the exact position he had earlier that night, dipping in under the canvas flap stepping forward, his gun at the ready, his eyes and nostrils flaring. A black bayonet was now attached to the end of his gun, its blade glistening with dried dog blood. My shift—and the movie for that matter —was ending exactly as it had begun. Except that now, the captain was outmanned. And outgunned.

"Captain," I said to him, clasping the pistol grip of the rifle so there was no mistaking my intention.

He smiled. A wide and honest grin. And for a moment, I thought that it would all be okay. That we would all walk away and laugh over a near-beer back at the morale tent. We would laugh and never speak or worry again about what might have been. But then the tent shook with the force of another pair of F-16s shooting through the sky above and the captain mouthed the words, "What are you afraid of?" or it could have been "Did you do what I asked you to do?" or even "Why are you pointing that gun at me? Don't you know that I'm not the enemy?"

He could have said any of these things in the deafening quake of war. But all I heard—clear and sharp over the peals of jet afterburners—was one word: *Draw.*

I swallowed and raised my M-16, almost imperceptivity. An awesome terror gripped me, mostly because Palmer had begun to laugh.

I turned to him. "Did you hear that?"

Palmer smiled back. "Sure," he said. "Can you believe it?"

"Hell yes, I can believe it," I said. "So what the hell's so funny?"

I guess you didn't hear me, Sheriff, Captain Moore said. But when I turned back to him, he was no longer Captain Moore. Standing there in front of me, squared off, was the bad guy from the movie. Decked out in black slacks and shirt, a black leather vest and stiff, wide-brimmed black hat.

"Jesus," I muttered, trying unsuccessfully to blink away the hallucination.

"Everything alright there, sarge?" I heard Palmer say. "The captain was supposed to kill that dog. Base hospital wanted one to test for rabies."

"Wha—?" I said, refusing to take my eyes off the man—the leering villain—in front of me.

The young airman was laughing now too, and I heard him say, "Jesus, sir, you had me seriously freaking. I thought you were one vicious bastard."

You draw your gun, the bad guy growled at me.

"It's still a crock of shit," Regina said.

Or by God, I'll shoot you where you stand!

"Are you guys hearing this?" I said. "Is anybody hearing this?"

And now Palmer had his hand on my shoulder, patting it. "C'mon, sarge. Ease up. Nobody here but us infidels."

Draw! the bad guy shouted.

In what appeared to be slow motion, the villain drew his weapon and I brought up mine, my finger probing deep into the trigger guard. And that's when I suddenly and completely remembered how the movie ended!

A blaze of gunfire. White smoke spewing across the saloon air like a bed sheet unfurling in the wind. Shrill cries of passion and pain and fear. Of war and religion and retribution.

Darkness came next. Then music. Sorrowful and ancient and forever.

Then credits. And copyright.

And finally *The End.* Written in fanciful script, signifying that a work of art, inevitable in its truth and violence, had just been witnessed and that now we were expected to retreat.

To forgive. To forget.

Now we were expected to live.

MAN SWALLOWS GOLDFISH WHILE SLEEPWALKING, CHOKES TO DEATH

My wife's family cornered the market on strange death. They invented the concept. They hold the freaking patent. To look up my wife's family tree is to see twisted branches filled with decapitations, puddle drownings, impalements, accidental hangings, circus animal attacks. You name it, it's killed them. Her own mother—God strike me dead if I'm lying—died from a sneeze. That's right. She sneezed and she died. I've seen the death certificate. Under "Cause of Death," the doctor wrote: *Coronary failure due to sudden, extreme, involuntary expulsion of air through nasal passage.* Which is a nice way of saying you died from a sneeze.

Of course, Susan never mentioned any of this to me before we got married. She seemed normal enough. There wasn't a dark cloud following her around wherever she went. She didn't have the Number of the Beast birthmarked behind her ear. Okay, so she was a bit uptight around the edges. She drove too slow, for one, hands always padlocked safely to the wheel in the 2 o'clock and 10 o'clock positions. But what woman isn't uptight? What woman doesn't drive too slow? Even when I visited her family— which boiled down to a couple of hefty aunts, an uncle, and two unmarried sisters—I never suspected a thing. We'd sit around the coffee table, speaking flawless in-law at each other. "Soooo," her sisters would coo, "how're the newlyweds?" "Fine, fine." "Still got that honeymoon fever?" "Uh, well—huh?" "Susan tells us you've been promoted." "Right. Assistant Store Manager." "My, my, aren't we on the fast track . . ."

But after a while I started picking up odd clips of conversation around the backyard barbecue. Things like, "Isn't that Grandma's scarf?" "Looks good as new, doesn't it?" "But I thought the boat propeller . . ." "Nope. Got tangled up in the drive shaft after she was pulled under . . ."

Pretty soon, the tragedies began to take on direction, like a wet road appearing through the fog, a road reflecting an endless series of *Ripley's Believe It or Not!* episodes. First, they let drop some of the less complicated deaths, like the uncle who worked at Van Camp's and drowned in a vat of baked beans, or the younger brother who got his head stuck in a vase and wandered out into oncoming traffic, or the second cousin who bore the distinction of being the only certified victim of spontaneous human combustion in the history of the state of Ohio.

Once I gained their trust, I started hearing the more elaborate cases, like the one about poor Uncle Wayne from Cleveland. On a hunting trip, he happened by the nest of an Eastern Coral Snake—the most poisonous snake in North America. It picked him out of a line-up of drunken bar buddies shambling through a snowy field and bit him on the tip of the thumb. Well aware of the family curse, Uncle Wayne immediately unsheathed a giant buck knife, pressed his hand onto a nearby stump and hacked off his thumb. A week later, he returned to the scene, bandaged hand and all, to look for the severed digit. To mock death, I guess. And damned if he didn't find that thumb. Except it didn't look like a thumb anymore. It looked like a purple golf ball, swollen with poison. So much poison that even the insects stayed clear. But seeing this gruesome object wasn't enough for Uncle Wayne. He started poking at the thumb with a stick. Turning it over. Oooing and awing at it. That's when the damn thing popped like a tiny water balloon, spraying poison into his eyes and mouth. He died within the hour.

Bullshit? That's what I thought until one of my wife's sisters produced a photo album filled with newspaper clippings. Page after page of headlines that could feed the supermarket tabloid industry for years. *Man Killed by Rabid Pig!* one headline screamed. *Satellite Falls to Earth, Claims Life of Farmer* read another. Yet another offered: *Local Woman Accidentally Strangled While Restringing Harp.*

The funny thing—the real tragedy in my humble opinion—was that neither Susan nor anyone in her family thought dying under such ridiculous circumstances was, well, funny. Their great-grandfather—a man none of them even *knew*—was killed by an exploding cigar gag that went horribly wrong. But there I go coughing up a chuckle when Susan related the story and you would have thought I pissed on the man's grave or something. I got the silent treatment for a month.

Eventually, I just steered clear of the subject of death altogether. I mean if I said something like, "I just heard that So and So was killed in a car accident," Susan would turn around and, without a hint of sarcasm, say: "Car accident? Wow, lucky So and So." But I soon came to find you just couldn't dodge death with my wife. She just wouldn't let the issue die, so to speak. Especially when it came to my desire to expand on our little twosome. To procreate the hell out of ourselves.

Me, I love kids. And as far as I could tell, so did Susan. I mean, I've got more nieces and nephews than can be genetically justified and my wife coddles each and every one of them. Which makes her a dream come true since I wanted as many kids as she could spit out. But she was having none of it. Whenever I'd bring up the subject, she'd come back with, "Why would I want kids? So they can see me get eaten by a shark?"

"Shark? In Ohio?"

"Or choke to death. So they can watch their own mother choke to death eating a . . . a pickle."

"You don't like pickles. Besides, you chew your food a hundred times over. I've seen it."

"You've seen it, but you never once wondered why. If you stopped to wonder *why*, you wouldn't keep asking about kids."

In a way, she had a point. I'm not much of a wonderer. When the day ends, it's ancient history by the time my head hits the sack. I never have second thoughts about anything, and I never look over my shoulder. Maybe that's what happens when you come from a family where people don't routinely get crushed to death by motorized garage doors. My family? We just die. Straight out, nothing fancy. We're lucky to land a blurb in the o-bits much less a headline. Ask me about my grandfather's death and I could tell you the year, maybe, but that's it. Hell, the old coot could still be alive for all I know. I just never thought about death long enough to take it the least bit seriously. A blessing if you ask me.

But Susan, she changed all that. Which, it so happens, turned out to be a blessing, too.

By the time our one-year wedding anniversary rolled around, I'd heard about a hundred strange death stories—each one a mini-excuse for us not having children, each one a tiny barb hamstringing our future. It got to the point where I started daydreaming about being a widower, which scared the hell out of me. Not because I didn't morbidly savor the thought of being free from a marriage that was grinding up on the rocks of paranoia, but because I'd probably never be able to live down having a wife accidentally drown in the kitchen sink while washing the dishes—or whatever.

It was about this time that Susan's maternal aunt decided she wasn't going to wait around for the business end of Death's joy buzzer. She was a baker by trade and there's no telling how many freaky ways you can go in a bakery. So the fifty-two-year-old woman descended the stairs to her basement, stood in the middle of the cold room and shot herself in the head with a .22 revolver. By all accounts, it would have been the least strange death in the family—had it worked.

The problem was that after she pulled the trigger, causing the gun to kick itself out of her hand, the bullet decided to misbehave—as only bullets in my wife's family misbehave—and traveled *around* her brain, exiting the other side and striking the fuse box which blew out all the lights in the house. Still alive, but without the gun or light, she groped blindly around the room in search of a way to finish the job. The coroner who worked the scene with detectives surmised that, based on the amount of blood smeared across the floors and walls, she had rummaged around for nearly an hour.

"In circles mostly," he told me, wearing the crippled smirk of a man who had, until then, thought he'd seen it all. My wife and I had been called down to the morgue to identify the body. It was my first time identifying a body in a morgue so I did my best to appear worldly and courageous. We stood in a hallway while the coroner answered all my questions with gruesome detail. He wasn't paid to comfort us, after all, and he didn't seem to mind proving it.

"It just doesn't make any sense," I said, not really trying to make sense of it, but confident that this was something a worldly and courageous person identifying a body in a morgue would say.

".22 rounds will do strange things," the coroner explained. "Even with two holes on either side of her head, she was probably as healthy as you and me—except that she had two holes on either side of her head."

With one arm clutched around my shaken wife, I asked him if the poor woman had simply died from loss of blood.

"Not at all," he said, as though conveying a ray of good news in an otherwise bleak story. "She came across an old boot eventually. She undid the lacing, tied one end to her neck, then felt her way up onto a chair and looped the other end around the ceiling pipes. Tied a great knot, too. What sailors call a spider hitch. Don't ask me how she managed it in the dark." He smiled, then looked at me as if waiting for me to ask him how she had managed it.

"She was a baker," I offered, pointlessly.

"The strongest of any of us," my wife said, fighting back tears. "She had to be in this family."

A pause ensued. We all stood there, nodding to ourselves. A young morgue attendant, whistling "I've Been Working On the Railroad," wheeled a corpse-laden gurney past us.

"So," I finally said, reluctantly, knowing I would regret it. "Is that how they found her? Hanging, I mean?"

"Oh, no," the coroner said, his eyes now alight with amazement. "The boot lace wasn't strong enough. It snapped as soon as she put her weight on it. She broke both her legs in the fall."

I winced and shut my eyes. "Jesus."

"Yep, I think she crawled around in the dark some more after that," he said. "That's when she must have found the mallet."

My wife had stopped crying at this point. She was holding *me* up now, muttering, "Wouldn't you just know."

"Based on the wounds," the coroner said, matter-of-factly, "I'd say she struck herself on the head about a dozen times—with the mallet."

"Thank you," my wife said. "I think I know how this ends." She was leading me away now, half supporting me. The sterile linoleum hallway of the morgue swooned and quivered. Everything looked wet and needlessly clean. As we walked away, I could still hear the attendant whistling, and the coroner talking to himself, "Unfortunately, it was a rubber mallet . . ."

It took me a couple of days to get a handle on the whole thing. I kept seeing the aunt's face in my dreams, battered and hopelessly frustrated, her tongue hanging out, eyes rolling around like a cartoon character, the dull whacking sound of the mallet keeping comical time. Through it all, my wife kept saying things like, "See? It isn't too funny when you're face to face with it."

But on the eve of the funeral, I found myself determined to regain whatever ignorance I lost, to put it all into perspective, to squeeze the positive out from an otherwise barren pulp. I knew our marriage was headed for the childless dump, but I wasn't giving up without a fight. I figured the time had come for an ultimatum. And I couldn't think of a better setting than the aunt's funeral.

We dressed up in our Sunday best on a cloudy Thursday, toting black umbrellas and grim expressions. We got to the funeral home early, which turned out to be a mistake. For some reason, there were three funerals going on that day and the mortuary lobby was clustered with mourners, lurching around looking confused and underfed. It had all the feel of an overbooked airline waiting area. We had to fight our way through to the viewing room.

There were only a handful of people collected there, in small groups on the outskirts of a sea of folding chairs with velvet cushions. Susan scanned the room but recognized no one. Most appeared to be elderly men in suits. Two of them were embracing each other in the corner. Pretty tight-knit these bakers, I figured. Then, in what I thought was a tension-breaking crack, I whispered to my wife, "Nobody's wearing a baker's hat."

"What?"

"Wouldn't it be great if they all wore those floppy white hats to the funeral?"

Susan pinched my arm and gave me a look that could have turned sand into glass. Then she half-dragged me toward a gaping coffin festooned with dreary wreaths, as if what lay inside was my ultimate punishment. When we drew up to the coffin, we froze and clutched each other. Susan was the first to speak."Good God," she gasped.

I stared down at the dead body for a long time. Finally, I said, "That doesn't seem like . . . her."

My wife shook her head in disgust. "I guess this is what happens when you—" she paused to clear her throat. "When you die like she died."

"What, you put on fifty pounds?"

"It's the make-up. You'd think they could have done something besides heaping foundation on. She needs more rouge."

"And a shave."

"I mean, I understand the circumstances, but if this is the best they could do, then someone needs to take a long look at their license to practice . . . to practice . . . oh, what's it called that morticians do?"

"Mortify?"

"And that wig. It doesn't even cover the top of her head."

"That's because it's a toupee."

Susan started to say something, but stopped. She turned to me. "What?"

"On her head. It's a toupee."

She pinched my arm again. I gave a little yelp this time and immediately felt the presence of someone standing beside me. Out of the corner of my eye, I could see a silver-haired man in a dark suit waiting patiently to view the body.

"You're just full of jokes, aren't you?" Susan said tightly.

"I'm serious," I said. "This isn't her."

"What are you talking about?"

"We're in the wrong room. This is a man."

"Wearing a dress?"

The mourner beside me leaned over and whispered sympathetically at us. "It was his favorite," he explained. "He asked to be buried in it."

Susan groaned with embarrassment, then pinched my arm a third time, a new record. We hurried out of the room.

Neither of us mentioned the boner to Susan's sisters who greeted us at the door across the hall. We made devastated with a few of the guests, then took our seats for a short ceremony by a hired-gun pastor.

"What do we reach for," he intoned from a podium, "when we run out of hope?"

Not a .22, I thought to myself. *And forget about that old boot.*

The preacher gestured over his head, to some undefined space on the ceiling. Then he narrowed his eyes and offered an "our little secret" nod. "That's where," he said. "Oh yes, my friends. The big guy in the sky."

He droned on like that for almost an hour. He seemed determined to play grief-stricken, but he only succeeded in sounding sleepy, on the clock. Throughout his speech, I kept thinking about what lay in store for me if I stuck it out with Susan. More funerals like this one, I was sure. Over and over again.

Things finally broke up about noon. On the way out, I stopped off in the john, hoping to fall behind the crowd streaming off to the local boneyard. The bathroom was as spotless as the morgue, with gold-plated faucets and motion sensor urinals. I almost expected to see an usher standing there offering to slap some musk on my face. I took my time washing up, thinking I was alone, when I heard a pair of shoes shuffle behind one of the stalls. The door lock slid open and out came the silver-haired man who had inadvertently tipped us off to being in the wrong room. He didn't flush the toilet because the only business he was doing in there was crying. I could tell by the way his eyes looked, all puffed up and spent, like a boxer who'd gone one round too many.

The old man tottered toward the sink, sniffling and patting at the jacket pockets of his suit as if he were looking for a lost wallet.

I toweled off my hands and turned to leave. That's when the man spoke. Without ever looking up, he asked, "Did you know Phillip well?"

Caught off guard, I stammered, "Me? No, I don't . . . Well, I mean, we just met. Recently."

"He made friends fast. That's how he was."

I watched the man in the mirror, washing his hands, the water drenching the sleeves of his jacket. I cleared my throat and said, "Do they know the, uh, what happened?"

The man took a deep breath and shut off the water. He steadied himself against the sink, not bothering to dry his dripping hands. "His heart," he rasped, shaking his head. "It just gave out. While he was sleeping."

"Peaceful," I said. I couldn't help but wonder if this guy was snuggled up next to him at the time.

"Yes," he said in agreement. He looked down at his hands, as if wondering why they were wet. "But does he know?"

I was more than content not to answer, to just keep edging toward the door. Then he looked up at me, eyes wild with confusion, with accusation. "Does *he* know it was peaceful?"

My mouth opened, but refused to answer, not knowing how to answer. Finally, I managed: "I don't . . . He could . . . I mean . . ."

"He must," the man said, not even listening to my gibberish.

"Sure," I said.

"How could he not?"

"Hey. You know."

"Right?"

"You said it."

That's when the man sucked in a quick breath and held it. I pictured him keeling over right then and there, collapsing dead across the marble sink. But instead, he groaned out and shouted, "Oh, God!" Then he spun and hurled himself back into the stall. I could hear him vomiting into the toilet. The whole room seemed ravaged by his grief, like a diseased, racking cough ravages the throat. I turned and hurried out, nearly colliding with the hired-gun preacher coming in the door.

"Oh, excuse me, son," the preacher said, hiding behind his practiced smile and touchy-feely eyes. "Is something wrong?"

"Is something *wrong*?" I answered derisively, as if it were all his fault. "Oh, you're wonderful, man. You're really beautiful. You should hear yourself say that. You really should. You'd die laughing."

A warm, spring rain was falling as we drove home from the burial. The trees and fields that sprawled along either side of the highway seemed almost blinding in their greenness. With a vengeance, the thought crystallized in my mind that my marriage wasn't much different than my surroundings. Lush and fertile on the inside, but surrounded and constantly pressed by the granite hopelessness of my wife's past.

I finally broke the silence with my decision. "It's time," I told her as if nothing else needed to be said, as if all that was expected of her was a simple "okay" or "no way."

"For what?" she said.

"For children. It's time for children."

She looked at me briefly, then turned away. "You must be kidding."

I sighed, shooting for mournful. "I saw a dead man wearing a dress today. I found myself trying to console his lover in the men's room. I'm beyond kidding."

"How can you expect me to bring a child into this?" she said, vaguely gesturing out at the gray clouds and green hills rushing past. "I mean, we can't even commit suicide right."

"Right? She's dead, isn't she?"

"You *know* what I mean." Her tone had no jest to it. No "very funny," no "ha, ha." There was only "back off or die" and it stank up the car like burning rubber, like some dormant female scent gland used by pre-humans to protect their young. I knew I was pushing into unknown territory, but if there was a reason for not talking about bringing a child into the world at that moment, I couldn't think of it. Besides, her dormant female gland had awakened my dormant male gland, the one that makes us expand our chests in an effort to look bigger and unmercifully stupid. I goosed the engine a little, then swooped brazenly into the passing lane, cutting off a Toyota Corolla as if it were a potential challenger that needed cowing.

"Do you have any idea," I said, nearly shouting, "how many botched suicides there are every year?"

She waved her hands dramatically. "Oh, let me guess. Millions."

"Thousands," I said although I had no idea.

"Okay, so? So what?"

I started to answer, but didn't. Running strictly on adrenaline now, I spit out, "Do you know what that man died of? Do you?"

"Who?"

"The man in the dress."

"Don't tell me. Heart attack."

"Sleepwalking," I said.

Susan let loose with a mighty bray of contempt in my direction. "Oh, and let's see, someone shook him awake and he dropped dead—which is a pity because that's the biggest no-no when it comes to sleepwalking, right?"

"Can I finish?"

"It's also the biggest myth. It's impossible to die that way."

My mouth dropped open and I almost lost control of the wheel. "Impossible?" I fumed at her. "You don't even know the meaning of the word! Your own father carjacked himself, got tangled in the seatbelt and was dragged to his death."

"He was changing a flat."

"Susan. Nobody changes a flat going fifty down the freeway. Normal people pull over first."

She stared straight ahead, her bottom lip trembling in anger or grief. "Normal people," she muttered.

"Look, I just want to finish telling you about this guy," I said, the story now tumbling out of my mouth as fast as my brain could invent it. "He was sleepwalking, okay. He was sleepwalking in his back yard and he has a pond there and it's filled with goldfish. Well, he slipped on some wet rocks and fell into the pond. That's where they found him. He was dead."

She had her arms folded now. A vein I'd never seen before stood out on her forehead.

"The thing is," I said, "he didn't drown. That's not how he died."

Susan opened her mouth and, almost imperceptibly, said, "Stop."

But I couldn't. I was counting down to blast off and couldn't abort if I'd wanted to. "They didn't find any water in his lungs," I said.

"I mean it."

"Not a single drop. You know why?"

"Don't say it."

A single hot tear spilled over and raced down her cheek, sliding beneath her jaw and disappearing into the folds of her collar. Maybe it was for her father, maybe for the man in the dress, maybe our marriage. Whatever the reason, I knew immediately how wrong I was. How cruel. How useless. How utterly boring. But even so, I said, "I'll tell you why. Because a goldfish—a harmless little goldfish—swam into his mouth while he was in the pond and he swallowed it. He didn't drown. He choked to death on a goldfish while he was still asleep."

She allowed herself to swipe at the tear trail across her face. "Sure he did," she said.

"That's what I was told. I asked and they told me."

She turned to me, squinting, struggling against the strangling roots of her own family history. "And do you think," she said, "that they loved him after that?"

"Who?"

"His family."

"Sure they did," I said. "Do. They *do* love him."

"You're wrong," my wife said. "They're ashamed. They hate him for dying that way. Just like I hate my father for dying the way he did. And my mother. And . . ." She lost it then. She gave up the ghost to her tears. Heaving and cavernous, shaking the car like a strong wind, putting that gay lover in the mortuary toilet stall to complete shame.

I drove and listened to her cry. I could feel my will buckling under this sudden counterattack. With abandon, I waited for a space between her heaves and threw out, "They *still* love him, okay? If they didn't—if they *didn't*—then they would have made up something. They would have lied."

She pressed both hands to her face as though to keep it from falling apart. Finally, she murmured through her fingers: "I never lied . . ."

And in that moment, I felt whatever fight I had collapse into itself, like an imploded building rushing to the ground. I knew then that I'd do whatever she wanted me to do. I'd say nothing or everything. I'd leave her tomorrow or stay with her forever. But mostly I knew that I'd do whatever I could to save her from a fate that looked, for the first time, all too certain. I'd shield her from lightning bolts. I wouldn't let her plug in the toaster or go camping or take aspirin. I'd invent a forcefield and keep it stretched around her, free of anything painful, anything strange.

And with that thought, I heard myself speaking to her, stating the obvious, the last gasp of a seemingly vanquished foe: "You're the most truthful, the most loving woman I know," I said to her.

"How can you deny that love to our children? How can you deny it to any living thing?"

My wife smeared the tears across her cheeks and looked up at me. "Okay then," she said, barely audible, a tiny voice that carried an epic, unexpected, and total surrender. "Okay."

CANNIBALS IN THE BASEMENT

 My wife invited them into our house, the cannibals. There were three of them. Charlie and Tom were brothers, two squat men with phlegmatic, darting eyes that always appeared desperate to escape the clutch of their faces. The leader was Reginald. Wanda introduced him as "Stitch" because that's what Charlie and Tom called him. To my wife, they were the interview of a lifetime, a sure number one bestseller that she had always dreamed of writing. To me, they were three fishermen who ate their captain and were now living in my basement.

"It was actually the first mate," my wife informed me later. "The captain went down with the ship."

Wanda had read their story in some supermarket tabloid (*"Just Like Chicken: Fishermen Recount High Seas Horror"*), tracked them down and found them unemployed and homeless in South Port—not an uncommon condition for someone living in the depressed fishing village and, I suppose, for cannibals as well. She saw no reason (the whole eating-of-human-flesh taboo be damned!) not to ply them with bus fare and invite them for a little exclusive in our cozy home.

I suppose there's a clinical term for doing such a thing. "Senior Moment" misses its vast scale. "End-of-Life Crisis" doesn't quite capture it. "Raging Senility" comes close. Don't ask me to explain how it came to this. Ours was a semi-happy, one-child marriage that had seen a few rough seas and lean years to be sure. But we were only thirty-two days—a month or so—from retirement, from liquidating our real estate and settling into adjoining rooms at the local overpriced retirement community—the Song of the Seniors Condominium Village. There we could frolic on the beach with Max, our border collie, suffer an occasional visit from Jessica, our bubble-headed daughter and Breeze, our born-out-of-wedlock grandchild, and rejoice that we'd made it to the finish line without retaining even the smallest stain of regret. Who needed the strangeness of strangers—infamous tabloid cannibals to boot!—at this point in our lives?

"Just give me thirty-six days with them," Wanda said after an exhausting battle of wills that ultimately—as always—went her way.

"Thirty-six days?"

"That's how long they were adrift."

I told her that I didn't get it. She responded that it wasn't important for me to "get it" since I wasn't doing the interviewing or the writing or the publishing. "Besides," she said, "they'll be here tomorrow."

"Fine," I said, crossing my arms and harrumphing as if I'd gained some important concession. "But I don't want to hear about any of it. For the next thirty-six days, I don't want to hear about how they fought the sea, the thirst and each other and how they fricaseed their best buddy to stay alive. I'll read the book. While I'm sitting on the beach enjoying my golden years. Deal?"

She nodded sadly as if she had *made* an important concession, and then we shook on it, the way older, semi-happily married people sometimes do.

With sea bags in tow, the cannibals moved in the next day.

I met them that night. Over a dinner of overcooked pork chops that were about as tasty as dried sponge. Overcooked pork chops were a Wanda specialty and incidentally, one of the reasons I agreed to live out my years at an overpriced retirement home. It was to be just the five of us at dinner. Wanda, the three cannibals, and me. My shiftless daughter was supposed to be there, but phoned at the last minute to say she couldn't make it. She had a date.

"Anyone you know?" I asked her as our guests were entering the dining room. I watched them through the foyer doorway, milling around the table, oohing and awing over the simple place settings.

"Cut it out, Dad," Jessica said. "He's a nice guy. You'd like him."

I held the phone closer and could hear the baby crying faintly in the background. "So what are you going to do with Wind while you're out with this future nice-guy-you-used-to-date?"

"It's Breeze, Dad. *Breeze*. And she's staying with a friend. Stop rolling your eyes."

"I wasn't," I said, rolling my eyes and peeking around the corner. The cannibals had just staked claims on their seats. Max, usually pawing over guests, was hunkered down in the corner, ears flattened, whimpering anxiously. "Just as well," I said. "I wouldn't want an infant anywhere near this place tonight. These guys'll take one bite of your mom's pork chops, snatch up the baby like a spring lamb, and scurry off into the night."

"Dad, please be serious. This book project is very important to Mom. She's really nervous."

"*She's* nervous? There's half a dozen steak knives on the table. How long before *I* start looking like a spring lamb?"

"They'll only be there for a month."

"Yes, a month," I snickered. "A month and six days."

After I took my seat at the head of the table—Wanda opposite me, the two brothers to my left, Stitch on my right—I decided to skip grace and other obligatory pleasantries and dove right into the ground rules. Like they were not to handle any part of my antique tool collection that I kept in the basement workshop. That nothing was free in this world, including electricity, so they had better be mindful of it. And finally, that while they had free rein of the house, the upstairs bedrooms were off limits.

"Nothing interesting ever happens up there anyway," Wanda said to break the tension. Everyone had a good chuckle over that.

I guess you could say I was a bit thrown by the general appearance of the cannibals. They were all scrawny, each a week or two late for a haircut, prematurely aged and looking decidedly on the "something" side of "thirty-something." Still, they seemed harmless enough. The two brothers were polite to a fault. A lot of "Could you pass the potatoes, please, Ma'am" and "May I please have some green beans, sir?" They didn't eye me hungrily. They didn't eat with their fingers, snarling and gnawing on the bones like hyenas devouring a carcass on the open veldt. Even Stitch was the model of civility. He spoke knowledgeably about the upcoming baseball season, looming taxes and his hopes of crewing one of the many boats running stripers in the bay. He looked me in the eye as he spoke. His stare had a bit of that far and away look, but I never once got the impression that he was about to hack a chunk of meat from my shoulder.

The small talk led Wanda into an old standby of hers, one usually reserved for Jessica's low-life boyfriends. "Now why aren't nice men like you married and settled down?" she said, hamming it with up a grandmother's wink. "You know, statistically speaking, married men live longer than single men."

I could have gone anywhere with this one. Instead, I decided on a harmless joke. "She's right," I said with a grand smile. "Then again, married men are a lot more willing to die."

I guffawed, so loudly that it took a moment to realize I was the only one laughing. As is often the case with bad dinner jokes—and to this day, I'm not convinced it was all that bad—conversation dwindled in its uncomfortable wake. And while I can't say I warmed up to our guests, I did go to sleep that night feeling better about the whole situation. Safer anyway.

Thunder jerked me awake at about midnight. I sat up, wincing at the cracking sweep of light that flashed through the room like the residue of distant bombing. I reached out with the dumb anticipation that comes from forty years of marriage and found that Wanda was gone. With annoyance equally instinctive, I pulled on my robe and made my way downstairs. Along the way, I stubbed my toe against an umbrella stand which sent me hopping ridiculously down the dark hallway. In the brief silence of pain, I heard my wife's voice: "It's okay," she was saying. "It's okay . . . Nothing's going to happen."

Limping, I eased open the basement door and crept down the first few steps. I could see the cannibals there in the half shadow of the open, sparsely furnished room. The three of them huddled together in the corner by an aluminum shelf of old Lucite paint. My wife sat perched on the nearby sleeper couch, notepad in hand. "What are you feeling?" she said.

The brothers were clinging to Stitch, on either side of him, pulling at his long-sleeved T-shirt, cringing from each silvery flash of lightning, their eyes squeezed shut as if in response to the stinging spray of the ocean. Only Stitch's eyes were open. Wide, dry and powerless.

"So fast," he was saying. "Gone so fast."

"The ship?" Wanda said.

"Too much water," he said. "Too much, too fast. It's upright now. Slipping under. Sealed over."

My wife scribbled furiously. "Are you in the raft now?"

I was about to bring the whole fantastic scene to a stop quicker than you can say, "Moby Dick." I was about to flip on the light and yell, "Nobody's in any goddamn raft! You're in my goddamn basement and you're keeping me awake!"

But one of the brothers cut me off with a scream: "Where's the captain!? Where's the captain!?"

And then Stitch's voice, as simple and unwavering as the pain in my big toe: "He never got out of his bunk . . . He never had a chance . . . We're all alone."

The guys at the sheet metal shop rode me for the blue ribbon. And all because I opened my fat mouth in a surge of camaraderie that seemed to happen more and more as my retirement date drew near. You'd think they would have cut me some slack, me with only a month left on the job. Instead they gathered around me in the break room during lunch, over-mayonnaised ham sandwiches clutched in their grimy mitts, coaxing a little more out of me until, without warning, I had said too much.

"No kidding? Curled up in the basement corner? Is that some crazy shit or what?"

"So did they start drooling when they saw your fish-white legs poking out of your robe?"

"Bet they already got dibs on that dog of yours."

"Oh, sure, they'll start with the dog and the next thing you know, his wife's ass is sticking out of the oven."

"Come to think of it, maybe they could stay at my house next."

"Tell 'em my wife's free for dinner anytime!"

Only Stan, the 'Nam vet who was a few laps behind me on the retirement track, didn't pile on. He just stared up at the decades-old union bulletin board as if there were something of interest posted there. "Can't tell you how many times I've woke up in a storm," he said. "To this day, I still do. Reaching for my rifle."

"They'll be reaching alright! Reaching for the barbeque sauce!"

For the next two weeks, I spent most of my time at work, tying up what seemed like thirty-five years worth of loose strings. The biggest headache was training my replacement, a young kid just out of college who didn't have the first clue. Every time he opened his mouth to say something, I could almost hear the moaning of his parents as they flushed tuition checks right down the toilet.

As a result of the overtime, I didn't see much of the cannibals, which was fine by me. My wife would give me a brief report each evening about the progress of the interview and her book. How she now had a good outline. How she already had twenty hours of tape to transcribe. Blah, blah, blah.

Sure, whatever, I would tell her. Just let me know when they're gone.

It was about this time—a good twenty days into it—that I first noticed food disappearing from the refrigerator. Grocery shopping generally bounced into Wanda's court. She was always quick with a coupon which won you points in my house. Still, I would have to be blind to miss what was going on.

First out the door was a three-pound honey-cured ham that I had earmarked for my Sunday afternoon Dagwood Bumstead sandwich. My wife explained that Jessica had come by and freeloaded on the ham and whatever else she could fit into the baby's diaper bag.

"Since when does she eat meat?" I said. "Last I heard she was protesting the plight of the chickens."

"No, honey, it was the terror of the turkeys," Wanda corrected. "And I think she took the ham for the baby."

"Christ, what is it, part-Rottweiler?"

"Or maybe one of her boyfriends. You know how she is."

Sure, I knew, I thought. But I also knew my wife.

That's why I came home early from work the next day, a Friday, and made the fridge my first stop. Sure enough, there was even more open space in what just a few days prior had been a stocked fridge. That's when it hit me. They were hoarding. The bastards were hoarding. What else could it be? I didn't know much about starvation, but I knew hoarding had to figure into the process somewhere. Wasn't that what the Donner Party did right before they fell on each other, hatchets a-flailing?

I left the kitchen and located Wanda and the three cannibals out on the deck. Wanda sat poised with her notepad and tape recorder like some cub reporter with a scoop. The three men sat side by side on a reclined lawn chair, soaking up the early afternoon sun, their faces fixed with the weathered, serious expressions of cannibals relating the particulars of their diet. Their lips moved frantically, but they spoke without using their hands, something I found odd.

Undetected, I headed downstairs, sniffed the cold basement room for trouble, kicked the pile of neatly folded blankets like it was the tire of a used car. I opened the closet door with care, half expecting an avalanche of pilfered groceries. But there was only the musty smell of cardboard boxes and old magazines. My 1922 Phelps-Collins table saw sat in the corner, perched on a four-legged, solid Pennsylvania steel base that you just can't buy anymore. I could see the tool was a bit dusty, untouched, but I walked over to it anyway. That's when I noticed a smattering of wooden matches on the floor. I picked up a few and immediately started sniffing the air again. I wondered if they were smoking some kind of loco weed. I'd found matches in my daughter's room when she was a teenager. Smoke enough loco weed and you end up with a kid named Breeze.

I took my case to Wanda that night while we sat up in bed, her scribbling out possible book titles on a notepad and me, re-reading a copy of *How to Keep the IRS the Hell Out of Your IRA*. Max was curled up in a ball at our feet, dead to the world. When I related my findings and suspicions, she stopped writing and stared down at the notepad over the rim of her glasses. I could tell, after about ten seconds of silence, that she was straining to think up something good.

"Pilot light I think," she finally said and started scribbling again. "The furnace went out—you know how it is—and I asked them to light it."

I delivered a hearty guffaw and then had to consider that the explanation made sense. That damn furnace was about as useless as tits on a Chevy. "Well," I muttered. "I don't want them lighting the furnace. Especially with matches. Jesus, they'll burn the house down."

"They're harmless."

"So was Mrs. O'Reilly's cow. Right before it kicked over the lantern that burned down Chicago."

"It was Mrs. O'*Leary's* cow, honey. And historians have already disproved that theory of how the fire started."

"Stop changing the subject. We were talking about the cannibals."

She let out a scolding hiss. "*Must* you call them that?"

"What else? The Shake N' Bake Boys?" The Brothers Shish Kabob?"

"How about human beings pushed to desperation? A desperation that comes from having death take you by the neck . . . and . . . and . . . You think *we'll* ever experience that? No, ours is a plodding journey, with Death taking years to find us, to sneak up on us."

I yawned, feeling sleep sneaking up on me. "Look, I just don't want them burning my house down before I can sell it, okay?"

"It was a religious experience," she said, and I could visualize the wheels in her writer's mind cranking out the literary sausage links. "A communion. A reckoning. A pop quiz of life and death."

"A pop quiz of *what*? Jesus, you sound like Jessica."

"One question after another, they had to answer. With Death's hand slapping at their faces to keep them awake . . . demanding their attention . . . their participation . . ."

"This is called telling me about it," I said, rolling over, putting the pillow over my head. "Exactly what you're not supposed to be doing."

But she kept going, speaking to her notes, to the room, to Max. "Where is the next drop of water coming from? From the storm on the horizon? A storm that will fill our leaky raft faster than we can bail? And who must die first so the others may live? Who is most deserving of life? The strongest? The weakest? Or should we leave it to chance? To fate?"

I pretended to drift off to sleep, but her questions—some of which she repeated several times—kept me awake until she ran out of breath. Until the words exhausted her.

I was kneeling in the crevice of the front bay window, tacking a warped baseboard back into place when my daughter drove up. Wanda was standing behind me, sipping a glass of iced tea. I sat back on my haunches and calmly watched Jessica get out of her car, a nasally Japanese import that I bought for her out of pity. She was wearing some kind of frilly, floppy hippy outfit that she kept having to readjust as she reached into the back seat. After gathering up the baby, she slammed the door and marched up the driveway. The car made one sorrowful jerk behind her, then rolled slowly backward, picking up speed and veering hellbent off the edge of the driveway.

"Oh my Lord!" Wanda shouted in a single puff of sound and rushed to the front door.

The mailbox was the first casualty. Wanda's favorite butterfly bush was the second. The car finally wheezed to a halt in the middle of the street, the remains of the mailbox dragging under the front carriage as if it were holding on for dear life. All I could do was shake my head and watch, muttering, "Well, at least she remembered to take the baby out this time."

I stood up, fighting a rusty stiffness in my knees, turned and nearly collided with Stitch. He had sidled up behind me, wearing a stained white T-shirt, a pair of cutoffs and knee-high socks. Charlie stood behind him like a kid hiding behind his mother's skirt, straining to look over Stitch's shoulder, even though there was ample room.

"I heard voices," Stitch said when he noticed my startled expression. There was a delicate, wary twitch in his eyes that I found soothing and threatening at once—mostly because I wasn't quite sure of its meaning. The look could have meant *I sure hope no one's hurt* or it could have meant *I'd love to gobble up your liver.* Who knew?

"You probably heard voices because we were talking," I said, and took a step back, rocking on my heels, trying to get the stiffness out before I made my next move. The last thing you want a cannibal to see is any sign of weakness.

"Is everyone alright?"

"If everyone wasn't alright," I said, irritated, "I would've been the first one out the door."

Drifting in from outside, we could hear my daughter yelling, "It's that damn parking brake again!" and my wife answering, "Well you have to set it, dear."

I offered up a knowing grin to Stitch as if to say, "women," but he kept his strained look and didn't smile back. I cleared my throat. "So where's your other partner in crime?"

"Excuse me?"

"The other guy. There's three of you, right?"

"Oh, you mean Tom," he said, then looked back at Charlie who quickly averted his eyes. "He went away. He couldn't stay any longer."

"Great," I said with a healthy scoop of sarcasm." I'm missing him already."

The task of disentangling and dragging the mailbox and brush out from under the car fell on my shoulders. And my knees and my back. By the time I reparked the car and went back into the house, tiny arthritic spikes of pain were prodding every joint of my body. Wanda and Jessica were seated on a couch in the living room. On the other side of the coffee table, complete with tea set and tray of sandwiches, the cannibals sat stiffly and looked about as interested in the conversation as sleepwalkers. Max was licking the back of the baby's head as it crawled around on the carpet, headed for the kitchen. Since I was apparently the only one who found this disturbing, I shooed the dog away and picked up the baby. Almost instantly it fell into a drooling slumber on my aching shoulder.

I sat down next to my daughter. I was waiting for someone—anyone—to thank me for my work. Stitch and Charlie hardly looked up. They just nibbled and nodded every time Jessica asked them a question which wasn't often. I thought she'd be enthralled, probably finding some kind of cosmic significance in what they'd been through and even try to recruit them into whatever cult she was pledging that week.

But she appeared a bit uncomfortable and even eager to chat it up with me instead. She was adjusting a small blanket between the baby's mouth and my shirt when she said, "Mom was just telling us that you two are touring the Song of the Seniors tomorrow."

I looked around the baby's head at Wanda. "Remind me to thank Mom for publicizing our schedule," I said.

"I can't believe you're really going through with it," Jessica sighed. "It still seems so incredible."

"We're retiring," I said. "We're not getting sex change operations."

"But the house, Dad. Aren't you going to miss the house?"

"It's just a house."

Stitch spoke up. "There is so much safety here," he said. "So much stability. So much security."

We all looked at him as if he had just launched into a soliloquy in Pig Latin. Wanda fidgeted, clearly making a mental note to put his quote in her book.

"Well, that's one of the fringe benefits of taking responsibility, Stitch," I said. "You get a job, make payments, build a life from the ground up. You don't take hand-outs or glob on to other people."

"Thank you, dear," Wanda said, leering at me. "We all know your thoughts on responsibility."

"You're both still so young," Jessica said. "Retirement homes are like, well, like big coffins. For the living."

"Talk to your father when you say things like that," Wanda said. "It was all his idea anyway."

This was unexpected. A single verbal body blow that made my heart catch, that made me straighten up in my chair as if rising to a barroom insult. I almost forgot about the baby and had to quickly adjust my grip before it tumbled over backward into the tea. I shot Wanda a hard glare, even though she wasn't looking at me, and was about to speak my mind when Stitch chimed in, coming to my defense.

He said, "Someone has to make the tough decisions. To look ahead. To the future. Where all the tough decisions take us."

"Goddamn right," I said. "What he said."

I sat and stewed, hardly listening to the remaining small talk, until my daughter announced she had to be going. I walked her to the car and helped her secure the baby, still fast asleep, into the car seat. When she turned around for a goodbye kiss, I made a show of fighting the glare of her outfit. "Last time I checked," I said, "the 70s ended in '79."

"They're coming back, Dad," she said. "Along with mysticism and astral traveling and reincarnation . . ."

"Please stop. With my luck, I'll come back as a mailbox. And you'll still be driving."

Jessica looked up at the house. "I'm worried about them," she said.

"Who?" I said. "The cannibals?"

"They're still starving. I can tell by the look in their eyes."

"They eat every night."

Jessica pecked my cheek and got into the car. "You can be starving for more than food, Dad."

"I wouldn't know."

"What's so funny?" Jessica said. I wasn't sure how she knew I was smiling since she was busy buckling her seatbelt and wasn't looking at me.

"I don't know," I said. "I thought you'd be more interested in these characters. I thought you'd find them . . . mystical and all powerful. Here you are telling me you're worried about them."

"I don't mean that I'm worried *for* them. I'm worried about their relation to . . . well, to you and mom."

"Huh?"

"Just be careful, okay?"

I smiled and winked at her. "When have I ever not been?"

It was only after she'd driven out of sight that I remembered I had wanted to ask her about the food she'd taken. Of course, there was something else now. *Be careful?* It was the first time my daughter said any such thing to me. It was the first time she'd shown the slightest bit of concern for either me or my wife. Or at least, the first time I noticed. One thing for sure, I didn't like the feeling. She was finally maturing, and despite my constant griping—all justified, I might add—I suddenly wasn't ready for it.

Another quick-moving storm swept over the neighborhood that night. I stayed awake, listening to the rain patter the roof-top, ready to snag Wanda by the arm if she tried to go downstairs and interview the sailors in their imaginary boat. But she was comatose, snoring mildly. I don't know what made me get up, but I rose about midnight, padded over to the window and looked down into the backyard where I had a clear view of the deck. And there they were. Stitch and Charlie. Lying shirtless on the deck. Spread eagle, on their backs, with mouths stretched wide open. They lay there, lapping and gulping at the rain drops splashing onto their faces. Distant flashes of lightning made their eyes glow like fanned embers.

Be careful.

When have I ever not been?

Our appointment at the Song of the Seniors didn't go as planned. We were only supposed to be there through the morning. A few legal papers to sign, a nice brunch in the campus restaurant, a visit to the design center to pick out the curtains and paint we'd be looking at for the next fifteen years. Wanda and I arrived promptly for our 9 a.m. appointment with Mr. Everett, the asso-ciate manager. He was late getting to work, his secretary told us. After I brazenly mentioned that I'd never been late to work once in thirty-five years, I asked if we could just walk around until Everett arrived. The secretary, a young, trophy blonde who was struggling to repair her jammed stapler, said that she thought it would be better if we waited.

"Of course you do," I said.

The secretary glanced at her watch and flashed a smile. "Shouldn't be more than a couple of minutes."

So we waited. In an overplanted reception room at the visitor's center. A picture window looked out past a row of streamers and windsocks, over the bleached white boardwalk that led down to the bay. We could see a few folks strolling along the beach, a scatter of sailboats on the water. The sky above was grayed over with thick clouds that resembled brain matter. Elevator music—which I genuinely enjoy listening to—elevated from hidden speakers behind the plants.

The "couple of minutes" turned into twenty. I could feel Wanda looking at me, anticipating a blown gasket, but I kept my cool, whistling and tapping my fingers to Herb Alpert.

When I couldn't take it anymore—the music and the waiting—I shifted my frustration toward our house guests, not minding that I was getting a little loud and keeping the secretary from solving the mystery of the stapler. I asked Wanda if she'd noticed we were short one cannibal. She mumbled that he'd gone away.

"Sure," I said. "Gone away. That's exactly what Stitch said. I suppose the captain went away too."

"I told you, it was the first mate. And you're overreacting. Don't you think I would know if something wasn't right?"

"You mean beyond the fact that three—excuse me, *two*—cannibals are living in the basement, hoarding food and who knows what else and, unlike the rest of the civilized world, drink rain water—as it's falling from the sky? You mean besides all that?"

The secretary looked up and smiled.

"It's just one more week," Wanda said.

"One more week, my ass! I don't like it," I told her. "Not one bit."

A voice—the unmistakable voice of a butler—sounded beside us. "I do hope you're not talking about our lovely little community here."

We stood up and there was Mr. Everett. He had the whole used car salesman shtick down pat, including a plaid sports coat and pompadour hair-do. The only difference between him and most car salesmen was about two hundred and fifty pounds of rolling body fat. I once joked to Wanda that he looked like he'd eaten a couple of Chryslers.

He pumped my hand and apologized with a regal bow. When I told him about my on-time record, he laughed and said, "Let's hope you stay that regular in retirement! I'm sure Wendy here will appreciate that."

"It's *Wanda*," I said.

"Yes, of course," he said, bowing again and sweeping a hand out toward the door. "Shall we?"

Pompous Ass, I thought. I'd never liked Everett, but until today, I foresaw his existence as, at worst, tolerable. Hell, I didn't expect to see him much after we'd moved in anyway. But suddenly, he permeated the place, an immovable mascot the size and shape of a small moon that was destined to appear at my side night and day. I kept having to correct him on things like my retirement date. My line of work. He even managed to call Wanda "Wendy" again.

"I must get one of those little recorders," he said, huffing as we made our way across a courtyard ringed with decorative white benches. His body odor, a stew of semi-expensive cologne and smoldering fat cells, kicked into high gear.

We had crested a small hill, headed toward the design center, when I noticed a tall building set off from the hospital. A low-slung orange roof top capped the structure. We'd been on the grounds before, were given the grand tour a couple of times—the down payment, check-clearing royal treatment—but it suddenly occurred to me that we'd never been inside the building with the orange roof. I asked Everett about it.

"Oh that's the hospital."

"No, not that. The building next to it. With the orange roof."

"Ah," Everett said, holding the door to the design center open for us, trying to catch his breath or think up a good lie, I couldn't tell which. "That's what we in the retirement home business like to call our intensive, intensive care ward." He laughed, his fleshy chin quivering from the strain of holding the door open.

"That's great," I said. "What do normal people call it?"

"Ah, yes, well, I guess you'd call it a, uh, morgue. Shall we?"

"Mind if I take a look," I said.

"Oh, I'm sorry. I'm afraid it's off limits to all but official staff. I'm sure you understand."

We spent the next few hours doing the paperwork polka, visited our rooms, even met with the in-house veterinarian about Max. At some point, probably lunch time, Everett's pager beeped and he lumbered off in the direction of the cafeteria.

As soon as he left, I told Wanda to mix it up with some of the locals while I checked out the morgue. She held back my arm. "But, didn't Mr. Everett say—?"

"Right, not to go there. Which is code for we've got something to hide."

I was soon following the labyrinth of hallways that took me from one end of the three-story hospital to the other. I had never liked hospitals much or the doctors who grew rich inhabiting them. Not because I was fearful of sickness or a good financial milking, but because I had never liked complainers and what hospital isn't stuffed to the gills with them?

By the time I reached the rear of the first floor, where the intensive care ward was located, I had uneventfully run a gauntlet of automatic double doors with signs that said things like *All Visitors Must Sign In With Admitting Nurse* and *No Unauthorized Personnel Permitted Beyond this Point.*

It bothered me that no one—not the nurses, not the Marcus Welby doctors, not even the bleary-eyed janitors—stopped me to ask what I was doing there. Just past a small waiting room was a sliding glass door that opened to a covered walkway. Another sign—missing only an admonition of *We Really Mean It Now*—warned me not to go any further.

I headed down the walkway, fought off a wave of dizziness from the strong scent of cleaning solution. As I pushed open the last set of swinging doors, I suddenly couldn't get the movie *Soylent Green* out of my head and half expected to find a grim processing plant inside—filled with sanitation workers serving up the dead to the dying. Instead, a near blinding light greeted me. The room was whitewashed and illuminated with powerful lines of florescent warehouse lights on the ceiling. A couple of unoccupied gurneys were parked to my left, next to a set of wooden double doors. A small line of orange chairs stretched across one carpeted corner of the room beside a lone vending machine.

"So this is the bright light everybody talks about, huh?" I muttered aloud, trying to joke away the fear stealing up my spine. Perhaps more eerie than the light was the utter silence in that empty room. The thumping of my heart seemed everywhere, bouncing off the walls, vibrating the tube lights overhead.

I took one hesitant step toward the wooden doors when a male attendant, dressed in a starched white lab coat and whistling loudly, pushed through the doors and nearly collided with me. He froze when our eyes met, then jumped backward. His expression turned quickly from surprise to annoyance. With a confident shrug and smart-ass sneer, he cleared his throat and asked me if he could help me with something.

I told him I sure as hell hoped he couldn't. Not for a long time.

I closed out the week—and my thirty-five-year career with Putman & Sons Sheet Metal—without any undue excitement. The company took to heart my entreaty of "nothing fancy" for the retirement party and spared every expense. They set up the gathering in the break room, threw some plastic cups and utensils from the prior year's Christmas party on the table and away we went. Soggy deli sandwich cubes from the corner market were on display as well as an ice cream cake that was so frozen it bent the only industrial strength metal knife in the building. The cake ended up sitting untouched and defiant on the table like a block of glacier flown in from the Flemish ice cap.

The company president, A. J. Putnam III, showed up with a few of his lackeys. He stood around looking irritated until someone asked him to make a speech. That's when he smiled, asked for a moment of silence, and zeroed in on me appreciatively. "Wow, forty years," he sighed. "Forty years of dedication. Forty years of service. For—" At this point, my supervisor tugged on his arm to correct him. With another big smile, he said, "Thirty-five, forty, it all ends up in the same place, right? In the Sheet Metal Workers Hall of Fame. Let's give him a round of applause, folks."

Most of the suits made for the door soon after the president. The rest of my co-workers milled around, pumped my hand, promised to keep in touch, and warned me not to do anything they wouldn't do.

I stuck around for a bit out of politeness and soon found myself sitting alone in the corner by the coke machine. Stan eventually shuffled over and sat down beside me. He gestured to the room with a jaded expression that said, *Helluva sendoff, huh?*

"So how's it going with your cannibals?" he asked me, as if everyone had them.

"They'll be gone in a week," I said. "What's left of them. I guess that's the one upside of having cannibals for house guests. Every day there's fewer of them."

Stan didn't laugh. "I went through what they went through. In Vietnam."

"What, you ate your second lieutenant?" Maybe it was the watery punch or an over-indulgence in Vietnam movies or whatever. But it wasn't the best time to be fishing for sympathy from me. I didn't want to feel sorry for anyone other than myself.

Stan fixed me with a serious stare. "It dawned on me the minute I stepped foot in that hell-hole . . . just like it hit them the minute they stepped foot in the life raft."

"And what's that?"

"Odds," he said. "Overwhelming odds."

"Of what?"

"Survival. Every day we live with overwhelming odds of survival. We no longer give it a second thought. The chances of us making it to the end of the day are astronomical."

"Wow," I said, looking at my watch. "Never thought about it like that."

"Sure, sitting home watching television we're more likely to survive than when we're behind the wheel of a car. But even so, 99% of the time, the pendulum never swings very far from certain life. But to suddenly find yourself facing certain death. To suddenly discover that you will be lucky—*lucky*—to see another sunrise. Human beings are no longer set up for such a reality. We're conditioned to live forever."

"Some joke, huh?" I said.

Stan nodded. "On us," he said.

My odds of getting home safe and alive were pretty damn good since by the time I hit the freeway, traffic was backed up like a clogged drain. From the east, what must have been the thirtieth thunderstorm of the month loomed in the form of purplish clouds sopping up the dusk. I found myself thinking, of all things, about drifting in a raft on the ocean, watching the fading light, tossed by persistent swells, arms like pasta from the constant bailing, dreading the black graveyard of night.

These happy thoughts didn't last long. By the time I arrived home, the downpour had started, heavy and oily from the humidity. The first thing I noticed upon entering the house was that Max didn't jump all over me. He didn't jump at all. He wasn't there.

"Where's Max?" I asked Wanda, seated at the kitchen table, scraping a yellow highlighter across the pages of a medical dictionary.

She shrugged, made a show of looking under the table, then slapped her forehead. "He ran away."

"He *what*?"

"Stitch took him for a walk earlier and Max got away from him. You know Max."

"Goddamnit," I said, tossing my rain-soaked cap on the table beside her. "It's pouring outside."

"He'll be okay," she said. "He'll find his way back. He always does."

She was right, of course. Max knew the neighborhood better than I did. But I had just spent the last two hours in traffic and I was wet and annoyed and my life partner hadn't so much as glanced up at me.

"Well," I huffed, "I know a couple more people who will be a-okay. Only they won't be finding their way back."

With a flourish, I stomped off to the basement and thumped down the stairs, Wanda hot on my heels.

Stitch was seated on the sofa bed. He was stuffing neatly folded clothes into a sea bag perched between his legs. Beside him lay a rain slicker and a knit skullcap. He didn't look up at me, even when I stood over him, grumbling and clearing my throat.

I was wondering what more I could do to announce my angry presence, when I noticed, resting on the edge of the table saw, a red dog collar. Max's collar.

I pointed at it. "Jesus Christ, what the hell is that?"

Without ever looking up, Stitch said, "The dog slipped out of it. I'm sorry."

"Stitch tried to catch him," Wanda said.

Now I was steamed. Over the top steamed. "I want you out," I said through a grinding set of choppers. "You and the other one! ASAP!"

Stitch nodded sadly, cinched up the sea bag and finally looked up at me. His eyes were those of a starving, abandoned child, shell-shocked and exhausted from fear. "He's gone," he said.

"Who?"

"Charlie."

Wanda pawed at my elbow, saying, "I told Stitch to stay one more night if he needed to—"

I leveled a hard stare at her. "Over my dead body."

"I don't mind," Stitch said. He stood up, swung the slicker over his back and gently tugged on the skull cap. "I was going to leave anyway."

"Damn right you're leaving," I snapped, stepping back to show him the way, determined not to let him think this was *his* idea.

"We can't send the poor man out in this storm," Wanda said.

"If it's good enough for Max, it's good enough for him!"

We followed Stitch up the stairs and out the front door. Without so much as a gesture of thanks, he drudged off into the rain and headed north toward the highway and the bay.

I turned to Wanda. "Get in the car," I said.

"What for?"

"We're going out to find Max."

She didn't protest or even grab an umbrella or hat. She didn't say a thing, even after we pulled out of the driveway and began circling the block. I, on the other hand, cursed and groused like an old pro, gesturing at each raking flash of lightning to demonstrate how terrified our family dog must be.

We had driven around the block twice and were well into the third lap when Wanda finally spoke. "I'm sorry," she said. "I got wrapped up in the book."

"Tell me something I don't know."

I glanced over and saw that she was crying, her face buried in her hands, her wet hair pressed flat against her head. "Can't you see what's happening?" I said, lowering my voice a notch. "You let those cannibals come between us. They've been hoarding food since they got there. Then one of them 'goes away.' Then the other one 'goes away.' Did you ever think about that, Wanda? Did it ever seem strange to you?"

"Are you suggesting," she mumbled through her fingers, "that Stitch ate his two friends?"

"No . . ." I said, realizing how ridiculous it was. "But the food. What about the food?"

Wanda took a deep breath, contemplative and bracing. "I took it," she said. "I took the food and threw it away."

I looked over and found her staring at me now, her eyes lit up and shiny in the dashboard lights. She said, "I was recreating what they went through. It was the only way I could learn the truth. Don't you see?"

I turned back to the road, tapped the brakes, made a left turn, kept going. My head swept back and forth, scanning the dark alleys between houses for Max. But I didn't really see anything. Hell, Max could have leapt on the hood at that very moment, belting out "Singing in the Rain," and I wouldn't have noticed him.

The woman next to me was insane. And I was married to her. The space between us had somehow become an ocean in one brief moment of conversation.

"I'm doing it for us," she continued, pleading and desperate now. "Their story is *our* story—the story of the rest of our lives. And now I see it. We need to change course! We need to stay in our house. We need to stay with each other." She coughed, struggling to keep her words audible and unbroken. "We can't give up on each other."

"Nobody's giving up on anything," I said. "And nobody's story is our story. Nobody's—Look, we talked about this. We planned this. This *is* our life."

By now, I had lapped the neighborhood four times and had seen nothing but a couple inches of rainfall and a waterlogged trash bag that vaguely resembled Max. I swung the car back into the driveway and cut the engine. I left the lights on. Wanda immediately slid over and put her arms around me, crying into my shoulder.

"I never told you, but I'm scared," she said. "I'm more than scared. I'm terrified."

"Of what?"

"Of getting old."

I reached down and took hold of her hand, felt how fragile and cold and helpless it was. "Got news for you, sweetheart. You are old."

"But what if you die. Before me?"

"Me die?" I said. I turned off the headlights. "Is that what you're worried about?"

"I can't watch that happen and go on alone. I can't."

"You'll still have Jessica," I said. "And the baby." In the sheet of rain riding over the windshield I saw my daughter's face as it was the day before. Concerned and serious, a glimmer of the real world finally twinkling in her eyes. "She's starting to grow on me, you know—even if she can't remember to set the parking brake."

"But I won't really have them," Wanda said. "Not in that place I won't. I'll be all alone there."

I sighed, then snapped my fingers. "I've got it! How about you die first and I'll stick around for all the gloom and doom and green jell-o."

Wanda laughed then, a small, compressed vibration on my shoulder that didn't contain any real happiness. Then she sniffled and released me. She wiped her tears with the palms of her hands. "I guess it would be better if we weren't."

"Weren't what?"

"Old," she said.

I sighed again. "Not much of a future in it, is there?"

And when she smiled at this, I knew I had her. That she was mine again. That I had somehow convinced her—just for a second of time—that we might live forever.

Later that night, after a quick examination of the basement—which was left meticulous—I limped upstairs, the joints in my knees alive with a raw and rusted pain. I toweled off and took my place in bed beside Wanda, listening to the distant thunder peals, to the undulating rain slap against the roof. I thought about Max, wet and huddled near the base of a tree somewhere, cursing me for not finding him. I also thought of Stitch and Charlie and Tom, each one alone, on a different path, but with the same damn storm following overhead.

Maybe it was the thunder or the melodramatic chill in the house, but a sudden fear squirreled into my heart. Maybe Max wasn't coming back. Maybe Max—or at least his choicest portions—were taking up space in Stitch's stomach. And maybe not just Max. I had joked about it before—half-joked really—but now my mind clamped down on the idea of it, the very taste of it. The taste of truth.

The digital alarm clock beside me shuddered, blacked out, then came back on, its bright red *12:00* blinking a distress signal. I got up and made my way downstairs. Just as I was about to open the basement door, I heard it. The muffled whining sound of machinery. The whistling sizzle of steel. I put my ear to the basement door. The sound grew louder.

I licked my lips, somehow drawing strength from this simple act, and threw open the door. I flipped the light on and called out stupidly, "Is, uh, anyone there?"

The sound, fat and now unmistakable, filled the basement. It was my antique saw, whirring away like a busted siren. By the time I'd reached the bottom of the steps, I realized I was in my pajamas and slippers, my only weapon a set of arthritic knuckles. But as I scanned the small room, I saw right away that I was alone. I edged up to the saw, still spinning in its overlap cradle, the safety hook dangling on a small chain beneath the metal base.

I pressed the shut-down switch and realized, in the heavy silence that followed, that the electrical jolt must have triggered the saw. On the doorknob of a closet was Max's collar. I shuffled over to it and felt something beneath my slippers. A splay of broken wooden matches lay scattered on the carpet. I picked up a few and realized that they had been broken well before I stepped on them. In fact, they had been finely snapped, each one a different size.

Jesus, I thought. They were drawing straws. Deciding who stayed and who went. Just like in the raft. Always in the raft.

Outside, a thin shadow stumbled through the rain across the basement window. I hurried to the wall and peered out. My childish fear was gone, replaced by its natural descendents, pain and embarrassment. The idea that Stitch had come back and might be trying to get into my basement, back into the life raft, stunted me with new anger. I rifled through my tool bench and grabbed a hammer, hurrying up stairs, muttering a refrain of "Goddamn cannibal bastard . . ."

When I shot out the front door, the hammer comfortable in my grip, my bathrobe flapped open behind me like a superhero's cape. I stepped off the porch and recognized what a piss-poor superhero I would have made. The rain instantly chilled me and by the time I made my way around the side of the house, I was cringing, shrinking, the bathrobe soaked through, one slipper lost behind me. Still, I gripped the hammer tighter, ready to get one mighty swing off if I had to.

"Hey!" I yelled at the sodden, tangled tree by the basement window. The sound was swallowed up in the rain and the grim yellow light emanating from the basement. "Get the hell out! You're not welcome anymore!"

The tree limb shuddered, lifted slightly, and drooped again. A squat shadow pushed out toward me. I raised the hammer.

And there was Max, looking as beaten and weary as I'd ever seen him. He slopped through the mud, bounded over the wet grass and snuggly wrapped himself around my leg, whimpering and shaking.

I immediately dropped the hammer and bent over him, his fear and relief palpable through his drenched fur. And as I crouched, whispering that he was a good boy and that it was going to be alright and that I didn't mean to yell at him and that he was home now, I felt compelled to turn my face upwards as if to thank God for a great, small gift. But I wasn't really thanking God. I was feeling the rain with my face. Feeling the clamor of it in my open mouth.

OUR DEEPEST SYMPATHIES

The boy watched the khaki-colored, government-issued sedan cruise slowly past him. He was seated on the curb just outside of the Officer's Club Pool, shaded by the awning. A light blue towel lay draped across his shoulders. His swimming trunks dampened the sidewalk beneath him. Through the open door at his back came the riotous sounds of splashing and children at play in the naked heat of summer.

The car's occupants—two soldiers in wheel caps—were turned toward the row of identical houses that lined the opposite side of the street. The two men appeared to be scanning the nameplates affixed neatly to each of the screened-in porches. After several taps on the brakes, the car sped up, turned right on Sheridan Road and disappeared.

The boy rose and patted himself off with the towel. He stepped over to a nearby bike rack and wrestled one of the bikes free. He mounted the bike and rolled forward to the rim of the curb, but did not leave the shade. Instead, he sat and waited and watched the road. The car soon reappeared, having circled around the block. The hot air rising off the asphalt made the car appear to be moving underwater. The boy examined the car more intently, concentrating on the faces of its occupants. The driver was white and the passenger was black. Both men wore green army dress coats. The boy could see that they were still looking at the nameplates and seemed to be arguing with one another until the black soldier pointed emphatically at one of the houses. The car swung into the empty driveway and parked.

When the two men exited the car, the boy saw that they were junior officers, in full dress, complete with polished shoulder boards, ribbons, and chrome unit insignia. They adjusted themselves and strode toward the house.

The boy pushed forward, bounced off the curb and into the parking lot. He winced as he entered the blinding afternoon sun and nearly lost his balance. By the time he peddled across the street and into the driveway, the two men had emerged from the screened porch and were returning to their car. The black officer was the taller of the two, but only because the white one had taken on a deflated, weary look as if the sun were riding him down. His face was densely freckled and sweating. Both men wore aviator sunglasses.

"You guys looking for the Mastersons?" the boy said as he drew to a stop in front of them.

"That's right," the black officer said. His voice was deep and carried through the heat. "You live here, son?"

The boy pointed back over his shoulder, past the pool parking lot toward a cluster of brick duplexes. The buildings were arranged around a static display of World War II-era anti-aircraft cannon. "See that 105 on the end?" the boy said. "My house is right on the other side."

"That's nice," the white officer said, but he was looking at his watch.

"Tyler's a friend of mine," the boy said.

"Who?"

"Tyler. Tyler Masterson."

The black officer leaned over and whispered into the ear of his partner.

"Ah," the white officer said.

"He's not here," the boy said.

"Thanks, kid. We figured that out when nobody answered the door."

"Major Masterson isn't here either. He's in Iraq."

The white officer started to speak, but the black officer cut him off. "We're actually here to see *Mrs.* Masterson."

"He flies helicopter gunships," the boy said. "Apache Longbows. They can fire over 600 rounds per minute and that's just their 30-millimeter cannon. They took out over forty tanks and armored vehicles in the first six hours of the war."

The white officer sighed and checked his watch again. "Shouldn't you be in school, kid?" he said.

"Red flag day," the boy said. "Too hot. They let us out early."

The excuse appeared to annoy the white officer and he turned to his partner. "Do they do that?"

The black officer shrugged.

"Where'd you get your combat badge?" the boy said to the black officer.

The man glanced down at his ribbon display, then removed his sunglasses and squatted until he was eye-level with the boy. "Where do you think?" he said with a good-natured wink. "Take a guess."

"Let's see . . ." the boy said, rubbing his chin pensively. "That one's the Armed Forces Expeditionary—which could be anywhere, but I'm guessing the Middle East. That one's the War on Terror Expeditionary—which could be Afghanistan or Iraq—and, let's see . . . that's a KCM, isn't it? For Kosovo?"

The black officer raised his eyebrows in amazement and stood up. "You know your medals, son, I'll give you that."

The boy peered up at the white officer, who looked bored and thirsty. The man had only a single row of ribbons pinned above his breast pocket. No combat badge. "Don't feel bad," the boy said to him.

"Do I look like I feel bad, kid? Is that what you think?"

"Frank," the black officer said in a cautioning voice.

"My dad doesn't have any good medals either," the boy said, "and he's a full-bird."

"Is that so," the white officer said. "What's your full-bird daddy do, kid?"

"C'mon, Frankie," his partner said.

"He's a dentist. He works over at the medical center. He never gets sent anywhere. We've only been stationed three places since I was born and two of them were New Jersey."

The black officer stepped forward. "Listen, son. We're here on official business so I'm going to have to ask you to run along."

He reached out to pat the boy on the shoulder, but before he did, the boy said, "I know why you're here. He's dead, isn't he?"

Both men looked at each other. The white officer shook his head, then squinted up at the sky with an expression of mild disgust. "Where the hell are all the clouds?" he said. "I can't believe there's not a single cloud in the sky." He looked back at his partner. "You want to sit in the car?"

"Not without AC," the black officer said. He turned and gestured toward the house. "Let's wait on the porch steps. At least we'll be in the shade."

When the boy got off his bike to follow, the white officer held out his hand. "Where do you think you're going?" he snapped.

"Let him be, Frank," the black officer said.

The two men walked over to the steps and stood just inside the edge of the shade. The boy pushed his bike after them, but remained in the sun. His trunks were completely dry now and had turned stiff as though heavily starched. His disheveled hair had taken on a green-tinted color. From several houses away came the gruff sound of a large dog barking. This was followed by a woman's voice yelling "shut up!" and the dog immediately stopped.

The black officer removed his sunglasses again, held them up, blew at the insides of the lenses, then slipped them back on. He looked down at the boy. "Any idea where Mrs. Masterson is, son?"

"Nope," the boy said. "My mom's at the commissary. She should be home soon. We can ask her."

"We?" The white officer mumbled.

The boy leaned against his bike and began to rock it gently back and forth. "You guys have a pretty tough job, don't you?"

"You don't even know what our job is," the white officer said.

"There's this boy I know at the base school whose dad was killed three weeks ago. An IED got him. He lived up on Colorado Street. I heard that when you guys went to notify his wife, she threw a plate at you."

The white officer grunted as if offended. "Not us," he said.

"You don't have to worry about Mrs. Masterson. She's real nice."

"Do we look worried to you, kid? Is that why you're bugging us?"

"Why are you letting him work you up, Frank?" the black officer said.

"Hey, you're the one that invited him over here."

"Me?" The black officer looked down at the boy. "Did I invite you to come over here?"

The boy shrugged. "And this other girl in my class, her dad got shot on the first day of the war. He died later when they were flying him to Germany. I didn't know that girl too well because her dad was enlisted. But she never came back to school. I think they kicked her family off post."

"No, son," the black officer said, in a way that sounded painful. "They didn't do that. Trust me."

"And Paul Shipley's father got sent home early, too. He was wounded in a fire fight outside Najaf. But that's not the same thing."

"Not the same thing as what?" the white officer said.

"Frank," the black officer said. "Focus."

"Focus," his partner said. "How am I supposed to do that? With this heat and this kid and nobody home . . ."

The black officer reached out and gently squeezed the white officer's elbow. "Just stay cool and rehearse the script in your mind. That's all you need to do."

The white officer sighed. "I thought it would get easier," he said.

"What?"

"This." The white officer gestured vaguely at their immediate surroundings. "*This.*"

"Who told you that?"

"Nobody. That's why I thought it."

"Wishful thinking."

"Obviously."

The boy was silent, waiting for the two men to finish. Then he said, "Major Masterson will be the first on the whole street to get killed. I guess that's kind of sad."

"You guess?" the white officer said. "What's that mean? You guess?"

"Keep it up," the black officer said.

"It's just," the boy said, scuffing the sidewalk with the heel of his bare foot. "It's just that Tyler has been a total jerk ever since the war started. He makes fun of me a lot because my dad's a dentist and his dad's a helicopter pilot. My mom says it's because his dad isn't here and he doesn't have any discipline."

"We could all use a little more discipline, eh Frankie?" the black officer said.

The white officer grunted again.

"I really didn't mind at first," the boy said. "But pretty soon, everything was 'my dad shot up an Iraqi column' and 'my dad knocked out a T-72' and 'my dad's gonna bring me back a gold faucet from Saddam Hussein's palace.' He used to say the only thing my dad could do in the war was rid the battlefield of tooth decay."

The white officer flashed a wide grin and slapped his thigh. "Man, I'm liking this Tyler kid already. Do you think he—"

"Check that damn smile!" the black officer snapped. "What's the matter with you?"

The white officer clamped his mouth shut. His cheeks visibly flushed and he cursed under his breath. "Sorry," he mumbled. "I wasn't thinking."

"Obviously," the black officer said. "Do yourself a favor and start. Think about the script. Rehearse it in your mind. Our deepest sympathies. Everything we can do, we will do. But no consoling. No touching. And no smiles."

"Right. Sorry."

The black officer crouched again and addressed the boy in a stern, but kind voice. "Son, I appreciate your concern, but you need to leave right now. We're here on very serious military business and you're distracting us, okay?"

"No problem," the boy said. "I understand." He adjusted the towel around his shoulder, threw a leg up over the bike and rolled it back and forth until he had turned around and was pointed toward the street.

"And son," the black officer said. "I wouldn't worry about what Tyler did or said. You should be thankful that your dad's here and not there. Besides, your friend was probably more scared for his father than proud of him. Sometimes people act like jerks when they're scared."

The boy looked over his shoulder at the black officer. "That's okay," he said, shrugging. "I'm not gonna make fun of Tyler or anything. But I don't think he said those things because he was scared."

The boy pushed off and pedaled away from the house. He crossed the parking lot, glancing sideways at the Officer's Club

Pool as he went. When he reached the static display, he picked up speed, circling around the giant gun. His wheels fishtailed in the gravel scattered at its base. He gazed up at the weapon's inert barrels pointed toward the cloudless sky and simulated its firing by hissing *toff, toff, toff, toff* through his pursed lips. After a few laps, he spun off toward a nearby duplex, coasted up the driveway and under the cool, dark shade of the car port.

He parked the bike and tossed his towel over the porch rail. He stuck a hand into his pocket and pulled out a bent stick of chewing gum, still in its foil wrapper. He examined the gum, as if considering whether it was worth eating, then finally slipped it into his mouth, chewing ruthlessly. "Thankful," he said between smacks of the gum. "Thankful."

As he walked back through the car port, a dark green minvan honked once and swung into the driveway, stopping at the edge of the car port. The woman behind the wheel waved at the boy and he waved back. *Thankful*, he mouthed.

The boy watched as the woman got out of the car. "Looks like somebody's been keeping cool in the pool," she said to him. She wore a gauzy white blouse and a pair of loose jeans. Her hair was pinned back in a bun. She adjusted her sunglasses with one hand and pulled open the side van door with the other. She reached inside and emerged with a paper grocery sack clutched in each arm.

"I got it," the boy said, stepping forward to roll the van door shut. As the woman turned, her eyes wandered out past the static display and street and lingered on the sedan parked in the Mastersons' driveway. The two officers were still standing in the shade at the base of the porch stairs, talking with one another.

"Who's that?" the woman said to the boy as he reached out to take one of the bags.

"Just some guys. Can I help you carry those in?"

"Who'd you say?"

"They're nobody."

The woman held on to both bags and walked absently toward the back end of the van, her eyes never leaving the two distant officers. The boy tried again to ease one of the bags from her grip, but the woman held on. The boy finally turned and looked. One of the officers, the black one, had stepped away from the porch and into the sun. He was staring back at them, his expression tense and curious. The white officer was talking to him, perhaps asking him what was wrong, but the black officer did not seem to hear.

The woman looked down at the boy, turned back toward the two officers, then the boy again. Finally she said, "Where's your momma, Tyler? Are those men there to see your momma?"

The boy didn't answer. He gazed up at her. A heavy silence, ripe and potent in the heat, settled into the narrow space between them. The boy began to grind his teeth. His face and cheeks and neck took on a reddish color. He clenched and unclenched his empty hands.

The woman's mouth dropped open. She hitched forward, then dropped to her knees. "Oh Tyler, honey . . ." she said, setting both grocery bags roughly onto the cement driveway. She reached out toward the boy, to embrace him.

But the boy did not allow this. Instead, he lunged toward her, raking her sunglasses from her face, trying to claw at her eyes. The woman screamed and pitched backward, her arms raised in defense. The boy screamed too, his eyes moistened with rage, and swung his clenched fists blindly at her head.

The groceries tipped over in the struggle and several boxes and cans spilled out at their feet. A single tangerine tumbled onto the ground and rolled down the length of the driveway. The tangerine picked up speed until it reached the sun-drenched asphalt of the street, then it slowed considerably, as if it were moving underwater.